C. Pearson

A Diary of Travels in Europe During the Summer of 1881

C. Pearson

A Diary of Travels in Europe During the Summer of 1881

ISBN/EAN: 9783337122485

Printed in Europe, USA, Canada, Australia, Japan

Cover: Foto ©Andreas Hilbeck / pixelio.de

More available books at **www.hansebooks.com**

A DIARY

OF

TRAVELS IN EUROPE

DURING THE

SUMMER OF 1881.

BY

C. PEARSON, M. D.

WASHINGTON:
JUDD & DETWEILER, PRINTERS.
1881.

A DIARY.

June 25.—Steamer Ethiopia left its pier North River at 3.30 p.m., for Glasgow, has 76 saloon passengers on board, day clear and cool, water calm and smooth. As we steamed away from the dock hundreds of handkerchiefs waved us good bye, until they and the land faded from our view, and the sun sank over the wide waters. Spent the night comfortably, the vessel making 10 knots an hour.

26.—Clear, with high cold winds all day; but making good time, overcoats and winter clothing in demand, our good ship rides the deep blue waves like a thing of life, other vessels seen at times in the distance. As I write a number of immense porpoises, probably frightened by the ship, show themselves half out of the water, they seem to be from four to eight feet in length. How do they subsist; or, what do they live on in this briny deep? I do not envy them their habitation, think they must be lonesome, it does well enough this pleasant day to sit here on deck and look over the country where they reside, they seem to have room enough but doubt if they have very agreeable neighbors. At 2 o'clock the sailors throw the line, and find the speed of the vessel to be 12 miles an hour. This line, with which the measure is taken, has attached to the end a tin or leather cup, or funnel-shaped shoe, from 4 to 6 inches long, with the large end next the ship, the line itself running round a reel held by a sailor; the end of the line with the shoe attached, is thrown in to the waves, the cup catches on the water the force of the ship rapidly unwinds the cord from the reel, while an officer holds a small sand glass, when this has all run out the line is drawn in and the knots counted, these knots are at equal distances on the line, and each one counts two miles though in speaking of the speed knots and miles are usually considered the same thing. At 5 p. m. a cold rain is falling but not much wind, too cold to stay on deck.

27.—After a good night's rest the sun rises clear and bright; morning cool and calm; water as still as restless old ocean ever is. At 7 the engine stops, and the cry of a man overboard brings all the early risers on deck. The sailors lower the life boat and are off, now on the crest of a wave and again below. I conclude as I look at them with a glass as they recede till they seem but a speck in the distance, that their task is hopeless, but not so, they reach him more dead than alive a mile or more away, and bring him on board, by which time he is revived. This was a steerage passenger about thirty-five years of age, who, being tired of life, had made his way to the upper deck and jumped over the railing for the purpose of "shuffling off this mortal coil." Whether his disappointment is satis-factory to himself or not, it was quite a success for the sailors. This is a delightful day, clear and calm.

> Blue roll the waters, blue the sky
> Seemed like an ocean hung on high.

Numerous vessels are seen, and whales let us know by their spouting, their whereabouts. Some of the passengers amuse themselves with various kinds of games, while others are sick and see no pleasure in anything.

28.—Was awakened this morning by the barking of
the Captain's dog, the little fellow has no other home than
the ship, and seems to enjoy himself here; he is a general
favorite amongst the passengers and makes friends with
all. I never before discovered music in a dog's bark, but
away out here in the trackless deep it reminds one of home,
besides the songs of two or three canaries, and baskets of
beautiful flowers make our ship appear more homelike.
As we near the banks of Newfoundland we find fog, and
the whistle is sounded every few minutes, the day, too, is
more like November than June, too cold for comfort on
deck, but with overcoats and four meals a day we manage
to keep warm. This evening we lost our little dog overboard, whether by accident or not no one could tell, but he
was seen to go, poor little "Spunk," we all felt sorry to lose
him.

29.—Cold and uninteresting day, passing the banks of
Newfoundland, wind high, and sea much rougher than
any day so far during our trip, weather hazy and misty,
but few vessels in sight, some small fishing craft that rock
and dip with the waves, wonder they do not capsize, and it
would seem that some one had, for something that appeared
to be the wreck of a boat floated by, but it seemed to have
been long deserted. Many are sick, and I wonder all are
not the way they have been eating for four days; our
course is nearly due east, and we are now about one thousand miles out, having made the following runs: 26th, 273
miles; 27th, 284 miles; 28th, 281 miles; 29th, 287 miles.
Time on ship-board is reckoned by bells, and days from 12
o'clock M.

30.—Cold, disagreeable day; one of the sailors says " there is a bit of a sea on." I thought so myself. It had been so long since I had been rocked in a cradle I did not take to it kindly. Then this rocks you endwise, sets you one minute on your feet, then on your head, gives you a few twists, and rolls you over a time or two to be sure you are rocked all over. I asked a professor of music to show me the fellow that wrote "Rock me in the cradle of the deep;" I wanted to kill him; he said he was looking for him himself. There was no storm without, particularly, the most of it seemed inside; I thought of what Valentine says on a similar occasion ; " first the ship hove up, then the passengers hove up." Most every one was more or less sick. We are now in mid ocean where they say these heavy seas are nearly always encountered.

July 1.—Day dark and rainy, not a wind storm but a fine, cold rain, with wind enough to make it disagreeable; weather slightly warmer and sea not quite so rough, but enough so to suit most of us. Notwithstanding the rough sea, we made the best time yesterday of any day so far, 291 miles. This was owing to the wind being in our favor and having the sails up. At 12 M. they report we are half way over, and many of us feel just that way—"half seas over;" for my own part, I am playing Tanner, have eaten nothing but one cracker for twenty-four hours. If I owned the Ethiopia, or in fact all the ships of the Anchor line, it would be a splendid time for some fellow to make his fortune, as I would sell out to day at a bargain, the vessel rolls as if it were drunk, and I guess we all must be.

2.—Another chilly damp day, as I look out over the

wide waters I can scarcely realize but that we are out of
sight of land *on a western prairie,* but there is no stopping
for wood and water, no new passengers coming on board,
or old ones getting off, no calling out " twenty minutes for
dinner," we hear the hoarse breathing of the engine, feel
the throb of its iron heart, and the heaving of its bosom
like some huge mouster of the deep, it never tires or stops
to rest, it has its work to do and it does it well ; there is fog
again to day, and the whistle is often heard, but the look-
out on the bridge walks his ceaseless rounds, and the pilot
at the wheel holds us on our course. A cold rain has been
falling most of the day, but without much adverse wind,
so that we have mad^ good time, 304 miles yesterday, and
302 the day befor^.

3.—Another foggy and chilly day but with fair winds.
See a few sailing vessels, but they seem to make slow
progress compared with our steamer, and some day, it too,
will be just as slow, compared with some other craft that
will skim these waves like a bird, and make this journey
in five days. We are only prospecting on the shores of
science; the great discoveries are yet to be made. Distance run to day 272 miles.

4.—Much the finest day out, but the first fourth of July
when, in my experience, heavy underclothing and overcoats were at all comfortable. At 9 o'clock, on the upper
deck, we threw to the winds the stars and stripes, had the
Declaration of Independence read, let the eagle scream,
and gave three cheers for the red, white, and blue, in which
we were joined by the generous Scots. Afternoon had dinner, toasts, and music ; God Save the Queen, Columbia

the Gem of the Ocean, &c. Misty, with slight rain again
in the evening; the sun does not set here till 8 o'clock, and
when clear it does not get dark till 9, giving only about
six hours of darkness; rather hard on gas companies, and
those who prefer gas to day-light. In twenty hours more
we expect to sight land, the north coast of Ireland; some
of our passengers will there leave us.

5.—To-day at eleven o'clock, the Captain tells us we are
in sight of land. We made 283 miles yesterday, and will
reach Glascow to-morrow. We are all anxious enough to
see land, but we require to be told that we see it for I
could discern nothing but a cloud or a fog-bank. The day
was not clear, and they have much of this damp, foggy
weather here, with chilly wind. At two o'clock, the clouds
clear off, the sun comes out, and we clearly see the coast
of Ireland, and pass quite near Tory Island which seems
to be nothing but a rocky promontory rising out of the sea
on which there is a light-house; the view here is beautiful,
but, I believe, when you have not seen land for a week or
two, it is always beautiful, however rough or rocky. The
green of Ireland now appears, though no sign of cultivation as yet is visible, for the whole northwest coast seems to
be a bold, rocky, barren cliff, in many places rising perpendicularly for hundreds of feet, against which the waves
of old ocean have dashed for innumerable ages; but as we
proceed on our way the face of the country becomes
changed. By four o'clock, as we near Moville, we pass a
north of Ireland watering place, called Greencastle, and
a more green and beautiful place, as seen from the boat, is
rarely to be found. From the high hills in the distance whose
tops are hid in blue smoke, to the water's edge, the whole

surface is dotted with white cottages, green plots, well cultivated gardens, hedges, castles, and ruins overgrown with
ivy. At Moville nearly one half our passengers leave us, and
here at six o'clock, from a Londonderry paper, we first hear
of the shooting of President Garfield. At eight o'clock
we pass the Giant's Causeway; it could not be very dis-
tinctly seen, but by a great effort I succeeded in imagin-
ing how a superstitious people might have given it its
name.

6.—Arrived at Glasgow at 9 o'clock A. M. The scenery
up the Clyde from Greenock is lovely, we pass Dumbarton
Castle which figured conspicuously in the Scottish struggle
for independence under Wallace and the Bruce. It is on
a high, and from the river a perpendicular rock, nearly 200
feet in height, and is now used as a fortress. Glasgow is
the largest city in Scotland, and claims to be the third in
size in Europe, containing over half a million inhabitants.
It is probably the greatest ship building city in the world.
Its old cathedral, mostly built nearly a thousand years ago,
is a marvel for strength and durability. Far beneath its
dark, chilly, dungeon-like basement lie the bones of innumerable dead whose names you read on the tablets above
them. How gloomy, desolate, and lonely, to be thus disposed of. Is not death itself cold and dreary enough
without this gloom and mildew? For myself, let me be
buried on the hillside where the free winds of heaven may
waft the perfume of flowers, and the song of the wild birds
above me; where the forest trees throw their shade in the
summer, and their withered leaves in autumn; these are the
columns in the temple of nature where I worship, and there
let me rest.

7.—To day I visited Ayr, the birth place of Burns. A part of the old cottage stands much as it did on that cold and stormy night, January 25th, 1759, when the bard was born. A little nook in one corner about six feet by four is pointed out as the spot, and a mark of repairs at one end, as the part of the wall that was blown in, making it necessary to remove the future poet when only a few hours old, to a safer and warmer abode. The walls of Alloway's "Auld haunted kirk," some two miles distant, are still standing, though the roof is gone, and it is now only a ruin, much frequented by sight-seers and relic hunters, in its old grave yard lie the remains of the poet's father and other relatives, while he is buried at Dumfries. The well, near which the mither of Mungo "hanged hersel'," is a beautiful clear spring in the hill-side, walled up like a well and filled to the brim with cold sparkling water that bubbles down through a shady grove of forest trees to where the "Doon pours down his floods." A little way above is the "Auld brig" over which Tam O'Shanter saved himself on that fearful night, when—

> A child might understand,
> The Deil had business on his hand.

No one crosses it now except on foot, whether because it is not considered safe, or to prevent the wear. I stood on the "key stane" and looked down on the "bonnie Doon" which still flows "amang the green braes" as in the long ago. A new bridge has been built a short distance above, over which the road now passes. The Burns monument, which is a kind of memorial hall, stands on an eminence overlooking the two bridges, a short distance below the new church which is nearly opposite the old one. This hall contains a number of relics of the poet, among which, is the Bible presented by him to Highland Mary at their last meeting; also, a lock of her hair, this, whether faded by time or not, is now very light in color, a kind of yellowish white. The old building in Ayr, now known as Tam O'Shanter's Tavern, is still occupied as a beer saloon, the room where he met his "drouthy crony," and from whence he set out on his perilous journey at the "Hour o'night's black arch the keystane," is much as it was a hundred years ago. His chair and that of his friend, Souter Johnny, are still there, and as ale is still dispensed by the proprietor, I should not much wonder if another Tam on some dark and rainy night should be in as good condition on leaving it to see ghosts and spooks, as was Tam of O'Shanter long ago, and particularly, as I saw not a quarter of a mile away a large man lying by the roadside "O'er a' the ills o' life victorious" while his wife threw her shawl over his face and a small child held his horse. Mauchline is a small town twelve miles from Ayr, and near this is Mossgiel farm where Burns lived four years and wrote much of his poetry; here are the fields where he ploughed down the daisy in the early spring and turned up the mouse in November. I procured a daisy from the former, and would have brought a mouse from the latter could I have found one, but had to be content with a few heads of red clover. The room where the poet was married, at the house of his friend, Given Hamilton, is a small apartment not more than ten feet wide by twelve long, and they try to keep it as it was on that occcasion as nearly as possible. But we must bid Burns, as well as the "Banks and braes of Bonnie Doon" good-bye. After this day's visit to his old home, I wrote the following:

THE HOME OF BURNS.

In this rude cot first breathed the bard,
  Who woke in one responsive strain ;
A thousand hearts in fond regard,
  Even o'er the distant western main.

His soul of song could warm the heart,
  Transform affection into rhyme ;
Till love and sympathy depart,
  'Twill echo down the flight of time.

Here's Irwin, Lugar, Doon, and Ayr,
  His inspiration painted so ;
Here Laverocks sing, and Hawthorns fair
  Bloom, as he saw them long ago.

Here's Mossgiel farm, and now as then
  The daisies bloom, and in their turns
The mice will build their nests, but when
  Will Scotland find another Burns.

8.—Visited Loch Lomond, Loch Katrine, the Trossacks,
Sterling, and Edinburg. The scenery around these places
is not only beautiful but historic as well. Ellen's Isle, mentioned by Scott in his Lady of the Lake, is an elevated
mound-like and romantic spot containing little more than
an acre of ground, or rather rock, it may have served the
poet as a theme, but I cannot see why Ellen Douglas or
any one else should want to revisit it often. The blue tops
of Ben Lomond, and Ben Leddi, are seen in the distance.
Before reaching sterling you see to the left the Wallace
monument, and a little further on, on your right near Sterling Castle is the statue of Bruce ; he stands with his hand
on the hilt of his sword which is partly drawn, looking
towards the field of Bannockburn which is not far distant.

Here is the old cathedral where Queen Mary was crowned, together with the old Bible and pulpit from which John Knox preached the coronation sermon. Mary was born at Linlithgow, an old town some twenty miles from here, on the road to Edinburg.

9.—Spent the day in sight-seeing about the beautiful city of Edinburg, almost every foot of which is historic. Here is the old castle, a part of which they tell you was built twelve hundred years ago. From the south side it would be impossible to gain access to it, as the rock on which it stands rises almost perpendicularly three hundred feet in height. Everything in and about it indicates that it was built at a time when peace was the exception, and war and defense the rule. Here kings were imprisoned, and from its dark dungeons taken to execution. No one, without seeing it, can form an idea as to what it was in its prime, or, even what it is to-day. It is now used as a garrison. Holyrood Castle with its massive walls, some of them six feet in thickness, still stands as it did in the days of Queen Mary and good " Queen Bess"; here the bedroom of the former is shown with its odd furniture, the bed on which she slept, and the room where *Rizzio* was murdered. These rooms, as all others in these old castles are small and dark and poorly ventilated, built for safety, not for comfort.

10.—Got to Melrose, 40 miles south of Edinburgh, at 9 : 30 p. m.; wrote my name in the register, and went to bed with no other than day-light; slept comfortably under two heavy sheets, four blankets, and one spread. The days are cool and clear, an exception to most of the weather here. They say it rains more than half the time. Visited Abbottsford, the home of Walter Scott; it is situated in a wild picturesque spot some two miles distant. The building, as they nearly all are in this country, is built of stone, and so many changes and improvements have been made, both on the buildings and grounds of late years, that it is questionable whether, if Scott himself returned he would not require a guide. The grounds are embellished with gravel walks, hedges, and wide-spreading birch trees, which give to the place the appearance of a cemetery, and as this was Sunday the stillness added to its solitude. What this old town may be on other days I know not, but, with this and Melrose Abbey, I concluded it would not be amiss to consider the whole place a cemetery where a hundred generations, including the present, are buried. The Abbey is one of the oldest mentioned in Scottish history, and is now a ruin; both grounds and building seem neglected, moss and ivy cling to the broken columns and arches, while the birds build their nests far up on the crumbling walls. Thus does time make all things even.

11.—Left Melrose last night at 10.30 o'clock; but not still dark. I objected to travelling at night, as I wished to see the country, but I found it made little difference, as a clear night here is about as light as a dark day, of which we have so many. On the way to Sheffield I saw men mowing in the meadow at half past three o'clock in the morning, and from the amount of work they had done, they had, evidently, been at it for an hour. Sheffield is a smoky old city with the usual high chimneys of English manufacturing towns. Here the massive stone walls of Scotland give place to the dingy brick. Arrived at Bir-

mingham at 6 ; Warwick at 9 a. m., and Strafford-on-Avon
at 2 p. m.; of the former there is little of interest to be
said, like all other manufacturing places it is dark and
smoky. Warwick Castle is wonderfully romantic, and its
surroundings very beautiful. Its age dates away back to
the days of the Crusaders, who brought and planted, they
tell us, the Cedars of Lebanon that now grow around it,
and which, from their appearance, must be a thousand
years old. It contains one table said to have cost $50,000,
and a vase in its conservatory over ten feet in diameter,
carved from a solid block of marble, and found in the
Tiber, near Rome. It is said to be the largest vessel of the
kind in existence, and is thought to be over 2,000 years
old. The view from the top of the old castle, over two
hundred feet above the Avon that flows at its base, is beauty
itself, but we must leave it for Stratford, the birth-place
and former home of Shakespeare. This old town would
doubtless long since have been hidden from public notice
had not England's bard given it immortality. The old
house where the poet was born stands much as it did
300 years ago. Like the one in which Burns was born,
it seems to have been a frame of wood filled in with clay,
the floor of each cottage is laid with stone, arranged without order or system, as is also the case in the house of
Annie Hathaway, the wife of the poet. The storms and
suns, however, of over three centuries have left their impress on these rude cottages, and as we view them to-day
we cannot help thinking that however unequally mated
mentally, he and Annie might have been, in regard
to humble birth they were nearly equal. The house in
which he died has been torn down, and a new memorial
hall erected near the spot. One large room in this is fitted

up as a theatre; it belongs to a company of which Edwin
Booth is president; it is mainly supported by donations and
contributions.　Shakespeare was buried, as was the custom
in those days, under the stone floor of the church in Stratford, where a stone tablet, a little north of the chancel,
bears his name, together with that strange inscription so
familiar to all, and about the authorship of which so much
doubt has been expressed; but a much better epitaph
would have been from Hamlet in regard to his father—

> " He was a man take him all in all,
> We shall not look upon his like again."

12.—Got to London last night, and attended the Medical
Convention to-day, the sessions being held only from 2 to
5 : 30 p. m.　No accurate conception can be had of London
without seeing it, for it is a world in itself.　Nothing but
steam can convey you through it in any reasonable time.
Only think of going shopping down town so far away as to
require steam cars, running at the rate of thirty miles an
hour, half an hour to take you where you wish to go.
They have steam on what they call the Metropolitan Roads,
but instead of being elevated, as with us, they are right the
contrary, as in nearly everything else, and run under the
ground.

13.—Visited Westminster Abbey, House of Parliament,
National Art Gallery, British Museum and Library.　In
this abbey lie the remains of their kings for the past eight
hundred years.　I inquired for the tomb of Richard III,
but the guide told me he was never buried with the rest,
but in a small church yard near where he fell at the battle
of Bosworth Field.　This is a most wonderful receptacle of

the dead; the tombs are old and grand. In the museum, one would suppose that a pair of everything that had ever been made in pairs, was to be found. Parchments musty with age, papyrus on which the ink is as black to day as when it was put there thirteen hundred years ago. Paintings by the old masters, and sculpture over 2,000 years old. Here is the celebrated Rosetta Stone which has served as a key to the hieroglyphics found on ancient monuments; it is like a large black slate about three feet long by two and a half wide, it is kept in a glass case. A lady, who seemed to be an antiquarian, was busy reading and explaining to a class, the mysterious inscriptions on the old tombs, and sarcophagi, while scores of artists, both male and female, from different parts of the world were sketching the various objects of interest. Hundreds of students old and young, many of them authors, were busy in the library searching out statistics and authorities; for anything in the way of a book that can be found anywhere may be obtained here.

14.—Went to-day to the South Kensington Museum, another wonderful collection of paintings, tapestry, sculpture, and a thousand things that represent nothing in heaven or on earth; the substance of which never had an existence except in the imagination of the artist. Here, again, are other painters at work copying from the originals; many of these were evidently Americans, some Germans, and other nationalities. Supposing that about everything in the way of art had been seen, I was not prepared on visiting the Crystal Palace to witness the whole thing repeated, only on a grander scale if possible,

2

for this is a little Paradise. America can never equal the collection of rare and ancient curiosities contained in these places, as these cannot be bought, and there are no duplicates—all we can expect is copies of the originals. Many stalls or booths for the sale of fancy articles are kept in the palace, and being desirous of getting a souvenir, and in need of a pocket comb, I concluded this would be a good place to buy something of English manufacture much better and cheaper than I could get it in the United States, so I paid a shilling for a small horn comb that I could have bought at home for nearly one-half less, and soon after saw on it the *eagle and stars*. Of course, I concluded I had not made a big thing by my purchase.

15.—Went to the Tower, this far-famed ancient State Prison where so many kings and nobles were once confined, and from whence they were taken only to lose their heads on Tower Hill, just above the Tower, and now pretty much built over. Here is the block on which the Duke of Kilmarnock and others were beheaded, the mark of the axe still being plainly visible. It was in a wing called the "bloody tower" that the Duke of York and the young prince were smothered by direction of their uncle Richard III. This room, as well as the one in which for so many years Walter Raleigh was imprisoned, is not usually open to visitors, and I was assured at every point we could not get in, but being accompanied by an interesting and good looking English lady, who was very pleasant to the officers in charge, and by the use of a few shillings, we were admitted. The room is small and dark with only one small window to admit light through its thick walls, it is kept as nearly as possible in its original condition, the floor (for it is on the second floor,) is laid with boards some eight or ten inches wide, and would now be considered a very poor job of carpenter work. A few years ago a winding narrow stone stairway was discovered leading to this room, by which it is supposed the murderers entered, this does not seem to be more than twenty inches wide, scarcely space enough to admit the body of a large man, and without a ray of light, but such mysterious passages are not uncommon in these old castles, both above and below ground, and in those days, to be condemned to the Tower was almost equivalent to the death sentence. The dungeon is one of the most remarkable things of the kind in existence, it is under ground, or in the basement of the building, and originally had no door, one has since been made through the thick stone wall, the only means of access having been from above through an opening in the arch some 25 or 30 feet from the floor, and it was only through this that light or air could be admitted,. The walls are of solid masonry, and here are 15 feet in thickness. This gloomy chamber is about 40 feet long by 20 wide, and perhaps 25 high to the centre of the arch, so that when a prisoner was let down here, all hope of escape must have forever vanished. Another part is called the Beauchamp Tower, and in this the walls are nearly covered by names and inscriptions cut in the stone, among the rest is " Jane," which was put here by the unfortunate Lady Jane Gray during her imprisonment in this room, in 1554. Visited Guild Hall where the city council and aldermen meet, and sat in the chair of the Lord Mayor, first telling the officer in charge that I was a republican, but he seemed not to be the least disturbed by the name. This hall is not usually open to visitors, but being accompanied by an English friend who was acquainted, we were admitted. This day the mercury noted 97° in the shade; said to be the hottest ever known in London.

16.—Went to Windsor Castle the home of the Queen. It is nearly thirty miles from London up the river Thames. The place and some of the buildings have a history and tradition, dating away back to the days of Julius Cæsar. The location is one of the finest that could well be found anywhere, and the view from the top of the round tower, is unsurpassed in England. The park stretching away over fifty miles in circumference, and containing eighteen thousand acres is finely laid out with groves, walks, and drives, one of which, as straight as line can be drawn, is over three miles long and bordered on both sides by two rows of elm trees over two hundred years old. Away in the smoky distance may be seen the old church where Gray wrote his Elegy as—

" The Curfew tolled the knell of parting day."

Also the former home of William Penn. This place has been the home of England's kings for over eight hundred years ; but on this occasion, the queen being at home, no visitors are admitted into her apartments. But the government soldiers, with their red coats, are still marching on their regular beats just as they have been doing for eight centuries.

17.—Visited the Zoological Gardens, a wild romantic place, saw the lions and other animals fed at four o'clock.

They seem to know their dinner time without a clock, and manifest it by their restlessness. The collection of wild beasts here, may be more extensive than that at Philadelphia ; but no finer, though they claim to have a pair of all the animals, birds, reptiles, and insects, on the earth. These gardens are not open to the public on Sunday, except by tickets from some member of the society, notwithstanding, hundreds of persons of all nationalities were here sight-seeing or sitting in the shade of the innumerable forest trees.

18.—At Hyde Park to-day ; this is an immense country in the heart of a great city, with forest trees, drives, walks, lakes, &c. Here is displayed in the cool of the evening the fine horses and turnouts of England, with liveried servants, and lady riders. There is a broad shady drive of probably five or six miles where hundreds of their finest carriages and teams are to be seen filled with the city's aristocracy, while on the other side, some fifty yards distant, there is another broad thoroughfare where hundreds of ladies and gentlemen are having a good time on horseback. The space between these two tracks is a shady lawn, where chairs for spectators can be had for a penny each. There can be no doubt that in fine horses the English beat us, but as riders they are complete failures. I did not see one graceful lady rider, while the men are perfectly awful ; they, probably, are obliged to ride much less than we do, which may account for the difference.

19.—Went to Victoria Park, a vast tract of land laid out in an odd way, a part of it, at least 25 acres, seems to be an old common with only here and there a shade tree.

It would make a good base-ball ground, and the boys were using it for what they called "cricket," much like base-ball. Other parts of the park are beautifully laid out with shady walks, artificial lakes, and flowery lawns. Scores of idle men and boys were lounging on the seats, or sleeping on the grass, while hundreds of hard-looking, dirty-faced children were amusing themselves in various ways, trying to persuade themselves they were happy. This park is, evidently, to the poor people of London what Hyde is to the rich. Visited one of the theatres at night, small audience, and a queer affair all through, and as everything here is contrary, and as we go up stairs to get in, of course, they must go down. They have female ushers, and sell the programs.

20.—Visited Kew Gardens, as they are called, but it is really another large and beautiful park, much prettier than any other in London. Flowers, shrubbery, shady walks, and green lawns for miles in extent, artificial lakes, monuments, &c., all free to the public. To-night, went to the academy of wax figures, the most extensive collection, and exhibition of the kind extant. The figures are all life size, each representing some personage, and dressed in the costume they wore, while living, or as nearly so as possible. One of the first on entering is a police officer, and looks so exactly as they do on the streets, that visitors ask him a great many questions which he cannot answer. One figure, of a sleeping beauty, attracted much attention, the bosom rose and fell as in the act of respiration, and as naturally as if in life. One old gentleman sat in a chair with spectacles, and quaker hat on, turning his head from side to side as something seemed to attract his attention. How accurate other likenesses might have been, of course I had no means of knowing; but those of Lincoln, Grant, and Garfield, were simply caricatures.

21.—A monument erected in commemoration of the great fire which occurred here in 1666, is over two hundred feet in height. I went to the top of it to-day, from which I looked out on the great city that stretched away in every direction as far as the eye could reach, a world in minature, with its hum, its smoke, and its spires; while the winding Thames in the distance with its innumerable shipping added to the beauty of the scene. Also went to Hampton Court, another large park, with its old castle. In the latter may be seen acres of paintings, some of which are more than two hundred years old, but the colors of which are still bright and clear. Ancient tapestry lines the walls enough to carpet thousands of square feet, all of which is made by hand, and of which it is said one person can only make a square yard in a year. Some two thousand persons have apartments in this castle, and yet the rooms filled with paintings and other curiosities, would furnish accommodations for as many more. Here are to be seen the bed, curtains, and furniture of Queen Charlotte, and other queens of the past, who, it would seem, from the length of the bedsteads, must have been very short, these being at least a foot shorter than ours of to-day, and are nearly square; but with high posts and heavy curtains, full twelve feet long, The grounds in the park are finely laid out, old trees. flowers, lakes, and walks; here is the celebrated bushy park, and that curiously constructed hedge of hawley called

the " maze," out of which, after a person has once got in,
it is almost impossible to find the way, without a guide
who stands on a platform commanding a view of the
grounds, and keeps constantly calling to one to follow the
lady with the red ribbon, and to another the white hat, &c.
This is thought to be great fun, and a few pennies are
charged for admission. One portion of the grounds seemed
to be intended for picnics, and hundreds of children were
having a good time with their plays and games. This place
is noted for a conference held here in 1604, the result of
which was an authorized version of the scriptures; here
Cardinal Wolsey held forth—

" Full many a summer in a sea of glory,"

and his hall is still to be seen. Henry VIII also spent
much of his time here, and robbed the land owners for
miles around of their property to convert it into a deer park
for his own pleasure and amusement. Hampton Court is
reached by steam cars in about one hour, and is about
twenty-five miles from the main part of the city, on or near
the Thames, as nearly all their castles are, in and about
London, and nearly everywhere you go you see the red-
coated subject of the queen on his beat with his musket;
but what use he is, or what good he does, no one can tell.

22.—Left London last night, and by rail and steamer,
reached Antwerp to day at 11 a. m. This is an old city
containing now about 150,000 inhabitants, though formerly
it was much larger. Here is an old house and shop where,
the Germans say, the first movable types were made by
Gutenburg, also, the tools and bellows with which he used

to work; but the same thing is claimed, I believe, for Straus-
berg. Some of these first letters are shown, and also copies
of the first books printed with them. Their Cathedral has
a spire nearly or quite 400 feet in height, and the building
is decorated inside with paintings by Rubens, who came to
this city with his mother to reside when only ten years of
age. Visited an old castle, formerly a prison, built in the
eleventh century, and used in the sixteenth for the con-
finement of heretics. By the aid of candles we descended
the narrow stone stairway that leads to the dark damp cells
below. Saw the iron collar and chain and staple in the
stone arch above, where, and in the name of religion, the
martyr was drawn up to make him confess. An old and
deep well now covered up, at the foot of a dark winding
stairway, was pointed out, where the captive in descending,
without any warning, stepped in and went to the bottom.
Other small stone vaults are here without light or air,
where the victims were confined till they were smothered or
recanted. And I thought of Ingersoll, and concluded with
him, if it had been my case, I would have said, " have
it your own way, one God or twenty, only let me out. On
the streets here women and dogs draw carts, and though
this old prison is no longer used as an inquisition, the progress of the people is dreadfully slow. The country through
Belgium seems to have originally been a bog or marsh, re-
claimed by drainage and embankments; the soil is produc-
tive, the crops consist principally of rye, wheat, oats, and bar-
ley; they were harvesting the two former, the grain is cut by
hand with sickles, and apparently every straw is saved;
the women do much of the work in the field. It is hard
to tell where one farm leaves off and another begins, as

they have no fences, and but few hedges. Their grain is
sown in small patches of one-half to two acres. No corn
is raised here, scarcely any in England, and I believe none
in Scotland; and certainly never can be if this weather is
a fair sample of the summers, for it is, one would think,
too cold to raise anything; still, potatoes are extensively
cultivated, and every inch of ground is made to produce
as much as possible, and the country resembles a series of
gardens more than farms. The houses which are usually
low, are built with a yellowish brick, and covered with tile.

23.—Arrived at Brussels at 11 o'clock a. m. This is a
city of some 200,000 inhabitants, and the capital of Belgium. The houses are principally brick or stone, plastered
or cemented on the outside, and painted a yellowish white.
The streets in the older part of the city are crooked and
narrow, the sidewalks being from twenty inches to three
feet wide. This is a great market for the manufacture of
carpets and fine lace., the latter is all made by women,
and by hand; and we may have some idea of how scanty
their wages must be, when a piece of lace that requires
their diligent labor for one week, can be bought for five
francs, about one dollar of our money. In the city hall,
I visited the room where the evening before the great battle
of Waterloo,

"There was a sound of revelry by night,"

as the ball was going on when the news came that the
French were approaching. In the art gallery they have
many fine paintings, some of which are 20 by 30 feet; some
of these henious representations, it is said, taxed the imag-

ination of the artist, whose name was Keizer, to such an
extent, that he became insane; and it occurred to me from
his work he might have been so before he began.

24.—Went to the field of Waterloo, which is about
thirteen miles nearly due south of Brussels. The drive
there and back is, for the distance, the finest I have ever seen.
One road is bordered for miles on either side with beech
trees planted at equal distances, and to all appearances
being two hundred years old. For another two or three
miles there is an artificial forest of these trees, which, al-
though their trunks are trimmed up some fifty feet, stand
so nearly together as to prevent the sun's rays from ever
reaching the ground. The combined powers have erected
on the field a huge earthen mound or pyramid two hundred
feet high, on the top of which is a monument with a massive lion looking towards France. But any one who will
take the trouble to examine the grounds may easily see
under what an immense disadvantage the French fought.
Had Napoleon occupied Wellington's position, the battle
would have terminated in his favor the first day. This field,
once enriched by the blood of one hundred thousand men,
except the old orchard where one thousand five hundred
men are said to have fallen in fifteen minutes, is nearly
covered by fields of wheat. On our return we passed over
a road built by Napoleon from Brussels to Paris, a distance
of some two hundred miles; it is straight, well graded, and
paved the entire distance with belgian blocks like a city
street, and I doubt if in all Europe Napoleon has a finer
or more durable monument than this.

25.—Got to Cologne at 11 a. m. This is an old, and once a walled city. It is on the Rhine, and was founded probably by the Romans as early as the fourth century; its population is about one hundred and forty thousand, and it is the capital of the Rhenish Province. Its great cathedral is one of its principal objects of interest, and it is indeed a most wonderful piece of mechanism, if not to say monument to superstition and folly. The arched ceiling in the center aisle is said to be 161 feet from the floor, and its cross nearly 400. In the church of St. Ursula, built some 800 years ago, they show you what they allege are the bones of 11,000 virgins, slain by the Huns over 1400 years ago for their faith in the holy catholic religion. From the time these virgins are said to have been massacred to the laying of the foundation of this church, a small interval of some 600 years, the history of these bones is not very clear. That they have a large collection of human bones here is very certain; where they came from, or to whom they belonged, remains in doubt. They also claim to have here a piece of the original cross, two thorns from the crown, and one of the urns that held the wine that Christ manufactured from water. That many believe these stories there is less doubt than that they are true.

26.—Left Cologne by railroad for Bohn, and take steamer on the Rhine for Bingen and Mayence. The Rhine is no wider, and perhaps, not deeper than the Allegheny at Pittsburgh, at least, no large boats are to be seen on it above Bohn. In many places its banks are cultivated to near the water's edge, while in others they are hilly and mountainous. These high peaks are in many places crowned

by the ruins of old castles erected many centuries ago.
High up on these beetling crags where it might be thought
nothing but the eagle would desire to build, but the same
motive that prompts the eagle to seek these inaccessible
cliffs, impelled the men of those days to do the same—self-
protection. On its hillsides, every available foot of ground
is utilized by the practical Germans, and the grape is extensively cultivated. Many strange and romantic legends
are told of the Rhine—its ivy-clad towers—its rocks and
hills; nor is this to be wondered at when we reflect that for
so many centuries all this picturesque country was the abode
of a superstitious and warlike people. I like to see such
ruins as are here to be met with, not because of their antiquity, but because a more advanced state of civilization has
made them what they are, and that time the great iconoclast
has dared to lay its hand on the follies of men, and in a
thousand years more the lofty cathedrals and costly temples
will crumble before the same power. " The mill of the gods
grinds slowly, but exceeding fine." It is difficult anywhere
to find finer or more varied sceney than on the banks of the
Rhine from Coblentz to Bingen. Byron wrote—

> The Rhine still nobly foams and flows,
>   The charm of this enchanted ground ;
> And all its thousand turns disclose,
>   Some fresher beauty varying round.

Coblentz is called the Gibralter of the Rhine. Its fortifi-
cation on a high rocky cliff overlooking the river and town,
is indeed a formidable looking place, and yet Napoleon
took it on his way to Russia. Bingen, at the mouth of the
Nahe, is not a large city ; it probably contains 8,000 in-

habitants who seem to be mainly engaged in the manufacture of wine, and what else could they do with their steep rocky hillsides than to cultivate the grape; and who but a German would have the patience to even do this. It was evening as we steamed up to the town, and of course we saw the sunlight shine—

> On the vine-clad hills of Bingen,
> Fair Bingen on the Rhine.

27.—Stopped a few hours at Worms, saw its cathedral, and bronzed statues of Luther and other German reformers. It is a quaint old city with narrow, winding, filthy streets, was once quite historic and contained five times the population it does to-day. Arrived at Heidelberg. at 3 o'clock p. m. The city is said to contain 22,000 inhabitants, but a city in the United States covering no more ground, would not have more than one-fourth this number. It is quite narrow, being confined between the river Neckar and the mountain covered by the "Black Forest." This mountain rises some 700 feet above the city, and covered as it is by this dense forest of pine, gives rise to its name. Heidelberg is noted for its University; and one of the branches taught here seems to be fighting. The students have a room about 50 feet long by 30 wide, where they go to fight with swords, the floor is stained with blood; their faces seem to suffer the most, and they may be seen by scores on the street with deep scars, which they seem to regard as a great honor.

28.—Heidelberg castle must have been at one time one of the grandest and most extensive in Europe. It stands on the mountain side overlooking the city, and perhaps 400 feet above it; and here part of it has stood for over 700 years, defying time, gunpowder, and lightning, though all of these have left upon it their impress. The French blew up part of it in the 16th century, and it was afterwards fired by lightning. It is now, and has been for a hundred years, a magnificent ruin; vines of ivy two hundred years old climb its walls, and trees as old wave their branches far below, and on the mountain far above it, one of its round towers, the top of which is reached by 150 winding stone steps, is still in a tolerable state of preservation; but few traces of its former grandeur now remain. One of its vaults was once used as a wine cellar, and in it are three wine bins or tanks, one of which is capable of holding 50,000 gallons, and is said to have been filled two or three times since it was built, it is 36 feet long, by 24 feet in diameter, made of wood in exact imitation of a barrel, the staves being eight inches in thickness. The castle has subterranean chambers, with dark winding stairways, massive stone arches and walls, some of which are 17 feet in thickness, these fill the beholder with astonishment but not with wonder that the same age that built the cathedrals should build these castles also; the former to solicit God's protection, the latter for their own, in case the former should be refused. But the men that built these have gone, and five hundred years hence the coming generations on a western continent can point with pride to a grander monument, and relic of the past, erected by their ancestors, and that, too, not a ruin, but to that temple of progress and reform, a country's salvation, the free school house.

29.—After a long but rather a pleasant day's ride of

over 200 miles from Heidelberg, by way of Stutgart, we reach Munich, another old town of nearly 200,000 inhabitants, and the capital of Bavaria. The country through which the road passes presents in many places the appearance of a western prairie, the absence of timber, except fruit and cultivated shade trees, adds to this similarity; no such thing as fences and very few hedges are to be seen, no country school, and very few farm houses, the people seem to live in villages and cultivate every available foot of ground; they sow and plant in narrow strips from twenty to one hundred feet wide, to fifty and three hundred yards long, a strip of wheat, another of rye, oats, clover, potatoes, and ploaed ground; all these and many more, with their varied colors, give the country the appearance of a cultivated landscape garden. Why they farm in this way I never could learn, the crops seem to be good, and as it was just their harvest, men, women, cows, and horses, were busy in the fields. But what they do with their grain is hard to tell as no barns or stacks are to be seen, they let the grain stand till very ripe, and probably thrash it with flails on the ground as American farmers did their buckwheat fifty years ago; at all events, in one instance, they were at work in this way. As we near Munich, spurs of the Alps are to be seen in the distance, their high peaks glistening in the setting sun like giant columns supporting the blue.

30.—The Iser river, on the bank of which Munich stands, is not so large as the Danube, which we cross at Ulm, on the way from Heidleberg; its water has a green color, and reminds one of the Green river in Kentucky. Visited the Royal Palace to-day, and it being Saturday, the King's private gallery of paintings was open to the public. The collection is fine, but intensely German, and with a German guide who could not speak a word of English, of course the *show* was not so interesting. In the National Art Gallery the paintings are more varied, and I should say much better, among others they have a representation of the surrender of Cornwallis at Yorktown, the stars and stripes look natural, but General Washington would scarcely know himself. The bronze foundry here is quite famous throughout the world, and some of their work may be seen at Washington, the east door of the Capitol, and statue of Lincoln in Lincoln Park. The statue of Bavaria is an immense piece of workmanship of this kind, it stands on an elevation overlooking the city, is a representation of a female crowned with laurel, and with the pedestal is nearly one hundred feet in height. The figure is well proportioned, and its head large enough inside to hold six men. This is reached by a narrow winding stair-way, and the ascent is made with some difficulty, and I was disappointed at finding the view so poor owing to the small size of the openings; the metal also, heated by the sun, made it very uncomfortable and somewhat dangerous.

31.—Spent this day also in Munich. The accommodations at the Hotel Bellvue are quite good for Europe, and whoever thinks it necessary to drink beer or wine while travelling in this country must except Munich ; they give you nothing for breakfast, however, but hard bread, butter, and coffee or tea, and as I drink nothing but cold water, of course my meal was rather slim. Sunday is a gay day

here, beer gardens, shops, stores, churches, and theatres are
all open, "you pays your money and you takes your
choice." But soldiers are to be seen everywhere, either
marching the streets with brass bands, filling the beer
saloons, or standing on the street corners; it would seem as
if half the male population of middle age were in some
way connected with the army.

August 1.—Leave Munich up the valley of the Inn
by Brenner Pass over the Alps, up, up at a grade of over
one hundred feet to the mile through dark tunnels and by
yawning chasms, until we reach an elevation of 4,000 feet,
with mountain peaks frowning down on us from every side,
whose bald heads hold in their gorges drifted snow that
glistens in the bright sunlight, and whose faces are furrowed by the torrents of many a score of centuries. We
begin to descend, and by eleven o'clock at night, after a
ride by rail of fourteen hours, arrived at Verona, in Italy.
Who has not heard of Verona, the tomb of the Capulets,
and former home of the Montagues? an old city located
on the banks of the Adige, and now containing about
70,000 people.

2.—The places of most interest in Verona are the Royal
Cathedral, the Church of St. Zeno, the old Arena, the
tomb of Juliet, and that of the Scaligeri, who lived and
ruled in Verona two hundred years before the Montagues.
The Cathedral, they tell us, has stood here since the ninth
century, but that the Church is much older, and that the
floor and foundation belonged to a monastry 1400 years
ago. The Amphitheatre is still older, and was built by

the Romans before the Christian era. Some four hundred
years ago a part of the outer walls was destroyed by an
earthquake, and the remaining portion seems to be in such
a good state of preservation that nothing less than this can
prevent it from standing forever. The massive stone steps
or seats, capable of holding 35,000 spectators, are still in
position, and standing room is afforded for 35,000 more.
The dens where the wild beasts were kept, as well as the
cells or dungeons where the gladiators were imprisoned,
before being called out to face these in deadly conflict, remain just as they were 2,000 years ago when this barber-
ous custom afforded amusement for 70,000 Romans. The
garden and old monastery, in which is pointed out the tomb
of the Capulets, or of Juliet, is most sadly neglected, part
of the building is used as a depot for storing the cocoons of
silk-worms. A sarcophagus in a small room, with stone
walls and floor, is said to be the one in which the fair
Juliet was laid; the lid is gone, and no sign of remains are
to be seen, there is an impression of a human form cut in
the stone bottom, but whether this was originally a tomb
or a bath tub is hard to tell, there are holes through the
stone, and it is said water once ran through these, and that
upon removing the lid centuries after the tomb was constructed, it was found the action of the water had decom-
posed, and washed away every particle of the remains.
This may not be authentic, but it is the story they tell.
The old romance from which Shakespeare gets his story is,
that in the days of the Capulets this building was a monastery, that Juliet lived here, and that in order to see her
Romeo scaled the garden wall; how he did this does not
plainly appear, as the wall on the inside is full twelve feet

in height, but then the story looses none of its interest on
this account; Shakespeare has told it, and told it well, and
the play that has made the place historic is here offered
for sale in four or five languages, and hundreds of cards
principally of Americans are to be found on the tomb.

3.—Arrived at Venice last evening, and went to our
hotel in a gondola, from which we stepped into the door.
What a strange city in the sea?

" The sea is in its streets."

It has but one railroad, and this has for two miles to be
built, like the city, through the water, on piles.   Venice
now contains 150,000 inhabitants, though it was once much
larger, and I predict that in less than 500 years more it
will be uninhabited, though it has stood here, or a part of
it at least, for probably 2,000 years.*   In fact, they show
you, in the Church of St. Mark, sculpture which they
assert was executed 22 centuries ago; two beautifully
wrought columns of allabaster, ten feet in height and ten
inches in diameter, are pointed to as having originally
been in the Temple of Solomon.   The ashes, too, of St.
Mark, the guide tells us, are here deposited, and his tomb,
or something that passes for it, is also to be seen.   A tower
300 feet in height, built some 400 years ago, stands near
the Church in the square Piazza San Marco, which is the
only public square, and is 200 yards long by 100 wide.

---

* There has recently been a proposition to fill up all but the grand
canal, converting them into streets, and to navigate the former by steam.
If there is money enough in Italy available to do this, the existence of
the city may be preserved.

From the top of this tower a fine view of the city and the
Adriatic, with its hundred islands, is obtained, and it is
stated that it was here that Gallileo invented the telescope;
and yet, as high as this tower is, Napoleon is said to have
ridden his horse to the top. This, at first thought, might
seem to be impossible, but the stairway, instead of being
steps and spiral, is an inclined plane, the grade of which is
probably four inches to the foot, full three and a half feet
wide, and as the shaft is square, and there is a level space
or landing at each corner four or five feet square, a horse
could easily make the turn ; the floor the whole way is laid
with brick. In this court or square, as the old bell on the
tower strikes two, thousands of pigeons flock to be fed.
We sat waiting for the signal, having been provided with
corn by the guide, and it was interesting to see how they
knew the hour, for scarcely had the sound of the last
stroke died away when they came flocking by the hundreds. No one is permitted to kill or even frighten them;
hence they are quite tame, and will eat out of our hands.
Every one has heard of the Rialto and the Bridge of Sighs,
and the latter, with its surroundings, presents one of the
most henious illustrations of cruelty and barbarity anywhere to be found. The canal over which this arch is
thrown is about twenty feet wide, and walled on both sides
by high buildings, one of which, a large, dark, massive
stone structure, with square, grated, windows, was once the
States prison. On the other side, and directly opposite, is
the Doge's Court Chambers, where those imprisoned for
treason were tried. In going from the prison to this
chamber they were obliged to pass through this bridge,
though from the inside it has no resemblance to a bridge, as it

is a dark, narrow, stone causeway, with only four singularly-constructed places, two on each side, where light can be admitted. These openings are a cluster of diamond-shaped holes, cut through the solid stone, and as the prisoners passed these, and looked out on the water beneath, they sighed for their freedom, without hope for their lives—hence the name of the bridge. After their trial, which, in most instances, was little else than a sentence, they were taken to the stone dungeons below, and this "infernal region," as it is well named, surpasses for inhumanity the most fiendish conception of men or devils. By the aid of tapers we follow our guide down dark, narrow, winding stairways to the subterranean arched caves or dungeons beneath. There are over twenty of these, perhaps ten feet square, with each one small, round hole, about eight inches in diameter, cut through the massive stone wall, to admit all the air and food to the prisoner, but no light as these do not open to the outer world, but to a passage as dark as the cells themselves. Here between their trial and execution they were confined, the door being closed. From this they were again taken still further down to, if possible, a still more diabolical place, where no daylight has ever entered, and after being tortured—the iron bars, &c., for this purpose still remaining in the walls—to make them confess, which, if they did not, they were beheaded and their bodies thrown through a hole in the wall, down which they fell to a spot where a gondola was in waiting to convey them to a certain locality for burial in the sea. Byron says:

I stood in Venice on the Bridge of Sighs,
A palace and a prison on each hand;
I saw from out the wave her structures rise
As from the stroke of the enchanter's wand;
A thousand years their cloudy wings expand
Around me, and a dying glory smiles
O'er the far times, when many a subject land
Look'd to the winged Lion's marble piles,
Where Venice sate in state, throned on her hundred isles.

The famous Rialto over the Grand Canal is a single
stone arch of about ninety feet span, and probably the
same in width. It is divided into three narrow streets, the
middle one of which is lined on both sides with shops or
stores. Close by this is pointed out the house of Shilock.
It looks more like a prison than a residence—has iron
gratings in its small, square windows. It was here that
Shakespeare has the old Jew say:

" Signor Antonio, many a time and oft,
    In the Rialto you have rated me
    About my monies and my usances."

Opposite, and within ten feet of Shilock's house, is
another old building, said to have been used for the first
bank ever instituted. The house of Brabantio, the father
of Desdemona, the wife of Othello, the Moor of Venice, is
pointed out as we ascend the Grand Canal. There are no
horses or carriages in Venice, and no place for them, or
streets wide enough for them to travel. I, however, saw
two of the former in a boat, and learned they kept two,
perhaps these, on an island near by, and that children who
had never seen a horse were taken there for that purpose.
The gondola is the carriage of Venice; there are over

4,000 of these, many families keeping their private con-
veyance as they would a carriage. The streets, for they
have some dry streets, or alleys, vary in width from three
to ten feet. These are very crooked, and seem to have no
names. They are paved with cut stone, as every foot of
space is, not built over. Not a tree, plant, or flower is to
be seen anywhere, except what are cultivated in pots.
The houses are built of stone below the water and brick
above, plastered and painted the usual yellowish-white color,
and covered with tile. They are from three to five stories
high, and most of the stairs and floors are either stone,
marble, or a kind of concrete just as hard and smooth;
hence, while there is very little danger of fire, there seems
to be very few facilities except water to extinguish it.
Their drinking water is brought a number of miles and
put in cisterns, which are only free to the poorer classes
two hours in the day, one hour in the morning and one in
the evening, and hundreds will congregate around these,
awaiting their turn; the crowd is so great as to require the
police to keep order, and many go away disappointed.
Water is carried through the streets by women, with two
buckets suspended from a stick across the shoulders, and
sold like milk.

4.—Visited the Art Gallery, which is said to contain
some of the finest paintings in Europe, but the eyes grow
weary of looking at so many miles of these, and at the same
conception of the artists transferred to canvas. I do not
believe I appreciate this style of art. I would rather look
at a live kitten than an imaginary dead Madonna; hence
I admire the human form in marble more than its shadow

on the wall, but the form that breathes and speaks most of all. This night a serenade was given on the Grand Canal to the Queen of Italy, who was spending a short time at the royal palace, and a thousand gondolas are out loaded with sight-seers. A large, square, fantastic-looking boat, built for the occasion, with awnings twenty feet high, and hundreds of colored lights of nearly every hue arranged in the form of festoons, carries the serenading party with music, vocal and instrumental, and after receiving the Queen on board we pass down the canal; this is about fifty yards wide, and was covered for half a mile with gondolas so closely packed that there was scarcely room for the oars. They pressed hard against each other, while the scream and jibbering of the gondoliers, the sound of music, the bursting of rockets, and the lurid glare from colored lights on the buildings, while the moon, nearly at its full, shed its faint light, all conspired to make up a novel scene like some enchanted fairy land. Such is "Beautiful Venice." A fraud on civilization, it was founded by fishermen in a rude and barbarous age for their own protection from rapine and plunder, but the customs of our times have no use for such a city, and its decay may be slow but none the less certain.

5.—At 12 m. to day we leave Venice by Bologne for Florence, a dusty ride by rail of nearly ten hours. Of the country between the two latter places a distance of probably sixty miles, very little can be said as so little can be seen, owing to the fact that one-half the distance is through tunnels in the Apennines, which rear their tall heads on every side, here and there a peasant has stuck his hut on the hillside, and attempted to cultivate small patches amongst the rocks on the steep mountains, but how any human can be contented to live in any such way is hard for an American to comprehend, particularly one who has spent many years in the prairie countries of the west. But these people have but few wants, and no aspirations higher than their fathers before them; the crucifix may be seen by the road side every few miles, and with this, they are contented; expecting a smoother country in the next world, they make no effort to better their condition in this.

6.—"See Florence and die" is an old adage, the origin of which is hard to ascertain, perhaps because some think this to surpass all other cities in beauty. It has, indeed, some fine scenery, and the Boboli Gardens belonging to the Petti Palace, are a paradise out of which no one would care to be thrown, particularly if afterwards he were obliged to cultivate for a living the dry barren mountains around here. The city lies in the valley, and on either side of the river Arno, and contains about 168,000 inhabitants; it is almost surrounded by the Apennines, whose smoky tops are seen in the distance. Here sculpture and painting have been long cultivated, and their collections of art in the galleries are so extensive as to weary and almost discourage the spectator in his attempt to see them. Over two hundred years ago Gallileo, who lived near here for eleven years, used as an observatory an old house that still stands on a hill overlooking the city. The church of Duomo, commenced six hundred years ago, is, it seems, still unfinished, as mechanics were at work on the south

side; it is a wonderful pile, and its dome is said to be
larger than that of St. Peter's at Rome; the money that
has been expended on it for the past five hundred years,
would, of itself, almost build a city, and educate, feed, and
clothe the starving poor of Italy; and yet within its sacred
precincts may be seen the zealous devotee, kneeling before
a crucifix, and muttering his prayers, while within a few
feet, and at the same time, the squalid beggar is asking for
alms.   So the world has gone, the more costly the churches,
the more ignorance, superstition, and beggary.

7.—Sunday seems to be but little observed at Florence,
stores and shops are open, and the unearthly yells of market venders on the streets, even till late in the night, makes
it difficult to determine whether they have something to
sell or are mad and fighting, for their scream sounds more
like the latter than the former.

8.—After a long, warm, and dusty ride of over 200 miles,
from Florence to Rome, we arrive at the Eternal City.   A
part of the country through which the road passes, seems
once to have been the bed of the sea, but now resembles a
kind of garden or orchard, with thousands of trees each
bearing a vine; but whether for this purpose alone, or the
double one of bearing fruit as well, I could not learn;
though they had the appearance of fruit trees, no fruit
could be seen.   Other portions of the country are broken,
barren, and parched with the drought, as it rarely rains
here in the summer months.   The climate though warm is
not oppressive, owing to the dryness, and the nights are cool

and pleasant; the hills are white with age, and their faces furrowed by many a weary century.

9.—Visited the Palatine Hills, where, crumbling to ruins you see the Palaces of the Cæsars. And what ruins! No description can be given so that a mind can comprehend their immensity, much less conceive what they were, when 2,000 years ago they shone in their matchless splendor. Sixty-three acres built over with massive columns, arches, and palaces above, and subterranean passages and vaults beneath. Many of these had lain for centuries buried from ten to twenty feet by the debris of crumbling walls and broken columns; but within the last century they have been excavated, and you now have a better idea of their magnitude. The Italian Government has control of all these historic places now, and a hired lackey with his sword clanking at his heels, is watching from a nook in some old wall, to see that no enterprising Yankee puts the whole thing in his pocket and carries it off. So here like the skeletons of some extinct race of giants, these frescoes, mosaics, columns, and crumbling arches lie, magnificent even in death.

10.—To-day I walked over the Forum whose broken columns had, for a thousand years, been buried beneath the debris of accumulated ages. I stood on the marble platform from which it is said Brutus and Antony addressed the Romans after the assassination of Cæsar, and viewed the spot where the excited populace burned his body; near by, too, on the left of the Forum, it is supposed Virginius snatched the knife from the butcher's stall, with which he killed his daughter. But the only auditors here to-day who witnessed these exciting scenes, is the dumb, cold marble, speaking only by its silence. For centuries the vandals have been at work amongst these ruins, carrying away the massive columns, and statuary to build and decorate churches and other edifices ; hence, it is difficult to find a public building in Rome less than three hundred years old, some parts of which have not been taken from some temple or building older still. The palace of the present King of Italy, has not an imposing exterior, and even inside is not as grand as one might suppose, as he has an annual income of two or three million dollars, but it contains some very fine statuary and painting, besides pictures in tapestry superior, perhaps, to anything of the kind to be met with anywhere, and, in my judgment, more natural and life-like than any oil paintings by Rubens, or Raphael. Rome has about 360 churches, and about three beggars for each church. One of these costly edifices, that of Scala Santa, has a number of marble steps inside, which, they assure you, are the identical ones from the palace of Pontius Pilate, down which Christ walked. No one is permitted to ascend them, except on his knees. I did not go up. In another church they show you piles of human bones that belonged to former monks. For many years, until recently, when a monk died he was buried in the earth in the basement of the church, this space was only large enough to hold forty bodies, and when full, and another grave was needed, the bones of the one first interred were taken up and cleaned, and now hundreds of these bones are artistically arranged on the walls in the shape of pyramids, stars, crowns, crosses, &c.

11.—As every body has heard of St. Peter's, we had set
this morning to "take it in." It is probably the largest
building of the kind in the world, being one hundred feet
longer than St. Paul's, at London, and in magnitude all
others are totally eclipsed, though in richness of finish and
beauty, St. Paul's of Rome outranks it. The top of its spire,
or cross that surmounts the dome is 426 feet high, the highest
point, it is said, ever built by man. I stood on the dome
and looked out on the scene below. Any one who has
done the same will know what I saw; none else ever will.
Here rolled the

> Troubled Tiber chafing with its shores,

as in the days of Cæsar and Cassius, the city spread out
on every side with church spires, columns, ruins, and winding streets, presents to the eye a sight rarely seen, and for
beauty of this kind, never surpassed. Not that Rome now
is itself such a beautiful city, it is not; but at such a great
height, the unbroken view, even away to the Mediterra-
nean ten miles off, together with the stupenduos and unequalled ruins, makes the scene unlike others, and only
such as—

> " The Great Empire of Rome can furnish."

This afternoon visited the Catacombs on the Appian Way.
This road of which so much has been said, was made, it is
thought, by Appius Claudius Cæcus (whoever he was)
nearly twenty-two hundred years ago. It is a straight
line for sixteen miles, but it is not, and never has been
graded with any skill or judgment, and in beauty and
durability does not begin to compare with the road built
by Napoleon from Paris to Brussels. It is so narrow that

it is with great difficulty that two carriages can pass each
other, and is up and down hill just according to the natural lay of the land over which it passes ; it was originally
paved with broad stones, but is now only a hard macada-
mized bed. For sixteen miles outside the walls of the
city this way was once lined on both sides with tombs, or
repositories for the dead. No conception of what these
were can be had from the name, but a faint idea may be
gained by stating that one of these, still standing, and
built for one woman alone, covers more than a quarter of
an acre of ground, and is, to-day, after having stood over
a thousand years, more than fifty feet in height. Few men
now care to spend so much money on their wives, either
living or dead, as did these old pagans. Let us give them
credit for their devotion to their dead, though they may
have had no well-defined ideas of any other world than
this. The catacombs, some two miles outside the city walls,
are a wonderful, gloomy, and dreary place. Each visitor
is furnished by the old monk, who acts as a kind of sexton
to the Church of St. Ignatius that covers the vaults, with
a lighted wax taper that looks like a piece of tapioca, and
down we go through the dark, narrow, winding passages,
like a coal mine cut, through a strange kind of dark soft
rock, in which all along, and branching off in every direction, excavations have been made just large enough for a
human body, in which, after it has been deposited, a marble
slab, or pannel, with name, date, etc., closes up the opening,
and thus by the thousands, one above another, five or six
feet high, they disposed of their dead ; but most of these
bones, as well as the marble panels, have been removed
to other places, leaving the excavations where they once

were, still in the rock. Some of these bones are now probably entombed somewhere, as those of St. Luke or some
other Saint, and I fear that they are so mixed that some
one may have trouble sometime to find his own, if he should
ever need them in a hurry.

12.—Walked through and over the walls and arches of
the Colliseum to-day, and it spoke to me in the language
of Ancient Rome; it told of the two thousand years it had
stood here, defying time and the destructive propensities
of men, of the hundreds and thousands of human lives
that had been sacrificed within its arena to gratify the
brutal propensities of the 80,000 spectators there assembled,
of the generations it had seen come and go, until its time
worn countenance plainly told it had become a stranger
amongst a race of men who knew it not. All this, and
more, in solemn silence was the story it told, and though
it has passed through so many changes, has been used as a
quarry to furnish building material for other edifices, its
old walls which measure over 20,000 feet in circumference,
and where unbroken, 150 feet in height still stand, and to
unborn generations will tell this old story over and over
again; and yet, as old as it is, and the great number of
churches and edifices it has contributed its columns and its
ornaments to build, many blocks of stone still remaining,
had at one time evidently formed a part of structures of
still greater antiquity, as their shape and carving had no
relation whatever to the present building, having in many
instances been covered by the builder entirely from sight
until the ravages of time revealed them. The Baths of
Caracalla, or all that is left of them, are perhaps more in-

credible and indescribable than the Colliseum. The walls
now standing resemble, at first sight, high clay hills or
mountains. The structure was a quarter of a mile square
its floors composed, or covered, with fancy colored mosaics
tastefully wrought in flowers and images, while its walls
inside were paneled with different colored marble and fine
sculpture. These old Romans then meant to keep clean—
one of the lost arts to the Italians of to-day—the aqueducts
of Nero, the columns of which are still standing, demonstrate
their appreciation of water, and how they left nothing un-
done to obtain it. I was somewhat surprised in passing
through the Capital Museum to have pointed out to me a
thin small beardless face as that of Marcus Brutus, and
another not much larger as Julius Cæsar, while a large
fine strong face with full beard they say is Caius Cassius,
and I thought, and still think that some Buttercup must
have mixed the babies, or somebody had blundered.
Shakespeare who makes very few historical mistakes rep-
resents Cæsar as saying to Antony—

> If my name were liable to fear,
> I do not know the man I should avoid
> So soon as that spare Cassius.

But the bust here is much larger and finer looking than
his own, besides a bust of Cæsar in another gallery has no
resemblance whatever to the first, so that little reliance can
be placed in either. But I leave Rome in the morning.
Good-bye, old fellow! I shall never see you again. I have
no doubt but, like many another, in your younger days,
you were handsome, but time has been busy with his work,
and the "Noblest Roman of them all" has long since dis-

4

appeared. May you renew your youth, and in the no
distant future be peopled by a' race of men with energy,
ambition, and enterprise.

13.—The country, by rail, from Rome to Naples, a distance of 150 miles, has for the most part, in August at least,
a barren and sterile appearance, is poorly watered, and in
many places looks much like a desert with mountains in
the distance. The grape here, as everywhere else on the
Continent, is largely cultivated, but the grain crop would
in our country be regarded as a failure. Naples is delightfully situated on a bay of the same name in the Medi-
terranean, and thought to be one of the finest in the world ;
it is the largest, and by all odds the most live and stirring
city in Italy. The population is nearly half a million.
The scenery is beautiful, stretching as it does along the
water's edge and up on to the mountain's side, from which a
fine view is had of the bay with its shipping, Mt. Vesuvius,
and other mountains in the distance. The idea generally
prevails that the city lies immediately at the base of the
volcano ; this is not the case. There is, of course, a good-
sized city all the way, but the main part of Naples is some
ten miles distant, though it does not seem so far ; neither
does the mountain appear so high until you observe that its
top is often lost in the clouds, which, when blown away,
leave only a column of white smoke, which rolls away as
if from an immense coal-pit ; but at night, when the red
flame shoots up, and the moon, slowly rising, reflects on the
still, smooth waters of the bay, the scene is grand, and as
for hours I sat alone and viewed it from the high balcony
of the Grand Hotel Nobile, I thought certainly this picture
must have been executed by one of the " old masters."

14.—I was much surprised at the climate of Naples at this season of the year. Who is it that has told so many stories and falsehoods about the heat, impure water, Roman fever, and other nonsense to frighten people, as they have about malaria at Washington? Were it within two hundred miles of the latter city I would advise people to go there as a summer resort to escape the heat. The mountain air and the delightfully cool breeze from the bay render the temperature pleasant twenty out of the twenty-four hours, and yet nine out of every ten persons, even those who have travelled on the Continent, tell you it is unsafe to visit Rome and Naples in July and August, or if you do you must- avoid drinking water, and it is a little strange that so many rather like to believe this. For my own part I had long regarded these stories as fallacious, and was disposed to test the matter for myself; so, instead of drinking no water, I drank *nothing else*, not even lemonade, tea, or coffee, and am well persuaded that those who pursue an opposite course, drinking wine and other artificial mixtures, are here, as elsewhere, the best subjects for disease. Were the people of any Southern city in the United States to live in one-half the filth, and in dark, narrow streets, eating and drinking miserable slops, as they do in these cities, one-half the population would die every year; but a dry atmosphere is always healthy, whether cold or hot.

15.—Saw and spent the day walking the silent streets of the once buried, and now partially exhumed, city of Pompeii. It is about fourteen miles southeast of Naples and four or five from the base of Vesuvius. Herculaneum is,

or was, about three miles nearer Naples, and also nearer
the mountain. Some 2,000 years ago Pompeii was partially destroyed by an earthquake, from which it had not
entirely recovered, when, 200 years later, it was totally
covered, to the depth of from twenty to thirty feet, by
cinders and ashes from the volcano. The idea prevails, to
a considerable extent, that it was destroyed by the molten
lava that flowed down the mountain's side. This was not
the case. The first shower that fell, to the depth of from
six to eight feet, was a kind of pumice stone, and probably
not heated; then some ten or twelve feet more of cinders
and ashes, buried the doomed city with most of its inhabitants, and so it has remained ever since, with the exception
of what has been uncovered. The Italian Government has
charge of the work, and, in their slow way of doing things,
may never finish it. It is now nearly a hundred years
since the first work was done; they are doing nothing now,
and have not been for two or three years. If they will
furnish the money, and employ Alexander Shepherd, he
will finish the whole job in a year. That it is a great task
to resurrect a whole city, there can be no doubt, and attended with much danger from broken columns and falling
walls. The part already exhumed is perhaps about one
mile long by one-quarter wide, as well as the amphiteatre,
more than a mile distant. Many of the houses have been
built with lava from previous eruptions from the mountain, and finished on the outside with cement and the same
inside, then either paneled with marble, or frescoed.
Much of the latter still remains, the colors still bright, the
representations of men, animals, flowers, &c., being well
executed. Of marble sculpture and columns there seems

to have been no end, as the old Romans appear to have
had a weakness in this direction. The floors of many of
their palaces, as that of Glaucus, the tragic poet, were laid
with mosaic, the colors and images still being bright. The
streets were paved with large, hard and irregular blocks of
stone not systematically arranged, and some idea of the age
of the city may be had when we find that these hard stones,
by the action of chariot wheels, have been in many places
worn in ruts from three to four inches deep. How many
years would be required to do this would, of course, depend
much on the amount of travel, but it was done before the
city was destroyed, 1800 years ago.

16.—The great event of this day was the ascent of Mt.
Vesuvius. This is accomplished principally by means of
carriages, about twelve miles from Naples, requires some
eight hours, and costs about six dollars for each person.
At the terminus of the carriage road, which is very good
and safe, but necessarily very crooked, we are drawn up
an incline plain, at a grade of about six inches to the foot,
by a stationary engine, some two miles further; here the
trouble of the whole journey commences.   Guides are
plenty who propose to assist you in various ways, for five
francs each ; pull you up with straps, or even carry you.
Some employ these guides, and some prefer to go it alone.
A few of our company got good, strong sticks, for which
they charge half a franc, (10 cents,) and concluded to ascend the cone about one hundred feet above. Seeing one
of the guides start, I concluded to follow, but soon found
myself in a dangerous situation.   The lava from a recent
eruption was hot, and the crust, in many places, so thin as

to be easily broken with my stick. Over acres this was of a bright yellow color, and thickly encrusted with sulphur, the smoke and fumes of which were so strong as to be almost suffocating. I concluded to find a cooler, and safer place. Arriving at the base of the chimney, or cone, we climbed slowly up, the ascent is so nearly perpendicular, and the sides nothing but a kind of loose ashes or cinders, that gives under your feet like pebbles, or sand; we slip back at least one foot in every three. Finally we reach the top, and look over into the seathing, boiling crater, still some fifty feet away, but near enough for all practical purposes. The volcano, for some days, had seemed to be angry, and threatening, and just at this time, whether for the benefit of the company or not, was giving a slight exhibition of an eruption, huge volumes of white smoke, and red heat were rolling upwards, and every few minutes a rumbling sound would be heard, and an explosion of gas from below would throw thousands of red-hot cinders hundreds of feet into the air, most of these fell again into the oven to be again expelled. After viewing this scene for half an hour or more, the showers becoming more frequent, and some of the burning cinders falling uncomfortably near, I was satisfied to call it even and quit, and to admit that, in an emergency, it was capable of carrying out to the letter everything it had ever advertised on its program. It is undoubtedly the oldest and most inveterate smoker on record, and uses the largest pipe. The view from the top of the mountain is superlatively grand, the green bay of Naples before you, the city to the right, Pompeii to the left, and Herculaneum, or where it once stood, just below. But I bid good-bye to Naples, a long and

last farewell. If its inhabitants have made any progress
in the past eighteen hundred years, is it any wonder that
Pompeii should have been destroyed? Let me give you
a little advice. We don't ask you to come to America, at
least not for a hundred years yet; but prepare yourselves
for this migration by adopting the customs of Americans
who come amongst you. Abandon your miserable style of
living, your villainous cooking, your hard bread and black
coffee breakfasts, your senseless *table d'hote* dinners of
which the following is a sample :

1. Soup.   (Colored water, vegetable slop.)
2. Boiled fish and potatoes, (without salt or butter.)
3. Roast beef and potatoes, (horribly cooked and spiced.)
4. String beans, (to be eaten alone of course.)
5. Stewed chicken and lettuce in oil, (chicken not done.)
6. Pickled peaches and grapes.
7. Uncooked peaches and pears, (never good.)
8. Cheese, (horrible.)

Whole time changing plates at table, one hour, no butter,
no salt in anything, and nothing cooked decently, hard
bread, no tea or coffee, plenty of wine and lemonade if
paid for extra; and this ridiculous custom is not confined
to Italy, but prevails all over the continent, and I would
only suggest, as an improvement on this folly, that each
bean be made a course, and each grape another. Why
do you not give your guest something fit to eat, and not
so many plates, knives and forks? Let them have soap
in their bed rooms, and use a little more yourselves; give
them gas, also, instead candles for light; cut down your
bedsteads about a foot, so that no one can be killed by falling out; have your hack and cab drivers stop their infer-

nal din of cracking their long whips; put a bit in their
horse's mouth instead of a barbarous brass or iron frame
on his nose, cutting the flesh at every pull of the line; let
your men have more ambition than to turn the crank of
a hand organ, or the tail of a donkey to guide him with
his heavy load through your narrow and filthy streets; let
your women prevent their four-year old children from
running naked through the streets, and quit wrapping
their babies up like mummies, or sacks of salt, leave one
foot out at least; let your laboring men, what few you
have, put on some clothing, and not go like South Sea
Islanders; have your soldiers pull the chicken feathers
from their hats, quit playing the fool, and go to work at
something useful—in short, have your country produce
something more than organ-grinders, soldiers, priests and
beggars.

17.—After a long and uninteresting ride of sixteen hours
from Naples, we arrive at Pisa, another old and played-out
town of about 50,000 inhabitants, situated on the river Arno.
The country from Rome to Pisa is not inviting, it would not
even make a good grave-yard, and yet it looks as though
it had only been used for this for the past century. As
the people live principally in villages, it gives the country
an additional desolate and deserted appearence. Peaches,
grapes, and olives are cultivated on the hillsides, and hemp
on the lowlands; upon the whole a thousand acres of such
land would be sufficient to bankrupt most men. The
absence, too, of singing birds, either wild or in cages, adds
to the gloom; and yet it is not to be wondered at that anything with wings should not be found here; bats, which are

very numerous, are about the only things that can fly and still remain.

18.—There is not much to be seen in Pisa except the leaning tower, that every child has heard of. It is well they have a leaning tower, for who would think of coming here for anything else. Many suppose this tower, which is almost 200 feet high and some 14 feet out of perpendicular, was originally straight; that owing to some defect in the foundation of one side, it has taken this leaning position; but this conclusion is not well founded, the column has evidently been built 'just as it stands, and is a fine piece of architecture, seven rounds of marble columns one above the other. If the original design was to demonstrate that it could be built in this way and still stand, the project has been a success; but if it was to add to its beauty, it was a grand mistake. As I stood on its top to-day and looked below, I wondered if my additional weight would be likely to topple it over; then I thought how many centuries it had stood here, and that if it fell just at that time, it would be the only way my name would ever be associated with it, but it showed no disposition to immortalize me in any such way, and as the old sexton was at the time furiously ringing one of its three huge bells without causing a perceptible vibration, I concluded it would stand a thousand years longer, and had not time to wait to see it fall. The road from Pisa to Genoa, one hundred and fifty miles, is a panorama of mountains, tunnels, and sea-side views. Genoa, where we arrived at six o'clock p. m., is another Italian city of about 145,000 inhabitants, and as churches and cathedrals seem indispensible, if not indigenous to this country, of course Genoa must have her's on exhibition.

19.—This city like most other Italian towns puts in its
claim for beauty, with its six story buildings and crooked
narrow streets, along many of which you could not wheel
a wheelbarrow and pass any one; but there is one spot, the
Catholic Cemetery, or rather depository for the dead, outside of the city, that is the most beautiful and novel thing
of the kind that I have ever seen, and must accord to whoever designed it the credit of originality, and expect some
day to see it imitated in this country, as I do not believe
any conception of it can be had without seeing it, I will
not attempt a description, but will venture the assertion
that it is the most complete burial place in the world, as is
its statuary the most beautiful in Europe. Say what you
will of the " old masters," the moderns beat them in everything, in design, in finish, in life-like expression, and in the
material used. Money is lavishly expended here by the
living on those who, during their earth life, possibly re-
ceived less kindness than now, but—

> " So runs the world away."

It cultivates, at least, that faculty which gave origin to
the belief in another world, or another life. The paintings
and sculpture in the churches here are only a duplicate of
what you may witness in other places all over the continent,
they are principally representations of Scripture scenes and
characters, and all wear the same sad and forlorn expression. I wondered if these are correct likenesses, and if
these personages have gone to Heaven looking just as they
are here represented, and I wonder also, if it is necessary,
in order to get into their company, to look just this way.
If so, I wish to be excused. Give me a happy smile and a

happy countenance, let me meet such either here or here-
after, and the storm cloud will be radiant with sunshine.

20.—Good-bye, Genoa! No wonder Columbus left
you in search of another and better world, I think I should
have done the same thing, though I should have drowned
in the attempt! The city seems to have a good harbor,
and a reasonable amount of shipping, but it can make
more noise for the same amount of business done than any
city in Europe. The country from Genoa to Turin, a
distance of one hundred miles, is better cultivated than most
parts of Southern Italy, and numerous farm-houses give it
a less desolate appearance. Still no country school house
is to be seen either here or or anywhere else in Europe so
far as I could observe. Turin is an old city, founded they
claim over two thousand years ago, and now contains some
200,000 inhabitants. What they all do, or how they all
manage to live, is one of the problems to be solved. The
mildness of the climate, however, renders their wants few,
and whoever would buy the wardrobe of one-half the
Italian people for one dollar a head would soon find himself hopelessly bankrupt.

21.—The most remarkable thing about Turin is its
straight and wide streets; remarkable, because it is such
an old city. Perhaps no other of half its age has either
wide or straight streets. The question arises, has it always
been so, or, owing to fires, has it been reconstructed? It
has many fine squares, with fountains and statuary. Of
course it has its cathedral and churches, which they claim
are not surpassed for beauty anywhere. They tell you, too,

they have in an urn in one of these the identical handkerchief with which Christ wiped his face while carrying the cross; this handkerchief is not on exhibition, but they assure you it is in there. The same story, however, is told you at St. Peters in Rome, besides they have two more in Italy, and three in France, making seven in all, and this weakens the story somewhat. In Rome they show you Nero's Tower, where it is said he sat and fiddled while the city was on fire, but those best informed say this tower was not built for 300 years after his death, and this completely destroys the effect. What a pity it is to spoil a good story in this way? We take no interest in the tower now, or in the handkerchief either.

22.—From Turin to Milan, about eighty miles, the country is better watered and better cultivated than any part of Italy I have yet seen; some corn is raised, as well as broom-corn and hemp. Milan contains over 200,000 inhabitants, and though a decided improvement on Genoa and many other Italian cities, its streets are by no means so wide and straight as those of Turin. It has its royal palace of course, and, seeing one of these in nearly every city, I was led to inquire if they had a king in every town; but it seems the king visits all these cities at stated times, and has a furnished palace in each. There are some seventy or eighty rooms in this one, all splendidly furnished. The ball-room has chandeliers of candlesticks, holding 3,000 candles; these are all in place ready to be lighted. Why they still persist in using candles in this way, instead of gas, not only here but all over Europe, is one of the things "no fellow can find out." They have gas in streets, in offices, and in many private residences, but in their churches, palaces, and hotel bed-rooms, you see nothing but the dim candle. Perhaps in another thousand years they will use kerosene, and in an additional thousand resort to gas, so that when I return again I may find this improvement.

23.—Milan claims to have the finest cathedral in the world, and, for its size, it is probably the most costly structure on earth. The expense of the marble sculpture and statuary, on the outside alone, would build four of the largest churches in America, and the work inside as many more. In a gilt circle, one hundred feet from the floor, in the arched ceiling, they tell you is one of the nails of the original cross. Twain says he thinks he may have seen a bushel of these nails in different places, but this is certainly not one of them, as it is not on exhibition ; they only point out the spot in the ceiling where, they tell you, it is. I greatly doubt if another such temple will ever again be built on this earth ; certainly not, unless the race is describing a mental circle, which, in the future, will again carry it into the delusions and superstitions from which now it is fast emerging. The inhabitants of Milan and northern Italy display more energy than those further south. There is more travel here also, and more life. This may be owing to the season of the year, for if the hotels of Pisa, Rome, and Naples have no more custom at other times than during the month of August, they would not make enough to run a good-sized peanut stand.

24.—Arrive at Arona, on Lake Maggiore. This is a

dead town, and ought to be buried. The lake resembles a river more than a lake. It is a long, narrow body of water, with, in many places, low banks, though in others the mountains approach the water's edge. The hotel accommodations here were the worst found in the whole journey, and the drinking water furnished was perfectly awful. There was certainly no excuse for this, as the clear water of the lake, only a few rods from the door, would have been much better. The hotel-keeper contended that it was unsafe to drink water at that season of the year, and I strongly suspected he gave us the meanest water he could find in order to induce us to buy his wine, but, as we only stopped here a short time, he made no great speculation. At midnight we leave Italy for the mountains of Switzerland in what they call here a diligence, and which it would require a good deal of diligence to describe. Each vehicle is intended to carry ten passengers. The body is constructed much like the old-fashioned stage-coach of fifty years ago ; then add a buggy-bed on behind and a carriage-bed under the driver's seat before, and, with four or five horses, the odd craft is off, looking like a circus bandwagon, on its way to meet another engagement. We *show* at Breg to-morrow evening at four o'clock.

25.—After an all-night and all-day's ride, we arrive at Breg, a small town on the Rhone river, in Switzerland, at the foot of the Tyrolese Alps. The Simplon Pass, over which the road leads, is a beautiful panorama of lofty mountain peaks, glaciers, cascades, cañons, and precipices a thousand feet deep. Some twenty-five miles of the distance from Arona a railroad might easily be built, but the

rest of the way it would be extremely difficult, if not entirely impossible. The carriage-road, however, the entire
distance, nearly 90 miles, is good, and, for horses accus-
tomed to travelling it, not necessarily dangerous. Whatever else they may do on the Continent, and through
Europe generally, in an awkward and bungling manner,
they can, and do, build good roads. But their diligences
are unnecessarily clumsy and heavy, being alone a good
load for two horses. Then two men must accompany each
one on every trip—the driver, and a man to look after the
driver, and do the *cussing* in Italian.

26.—Martigny is another played-out town, with nothing to interest any one except the Durand Cascades, some
five miles up in the mountain gorges. It is well for the town
these cascades are there. They were there myriads of years
before the town was, and probably suggested the idea of
building the town here in the first place, and they certainly
seem to be the means of keeping up the place, for nowhere
on the Continent have the hotels appeared to be better patronized, and teams are much in demand to visit this strange,
wild, and romantic place. After going by carriage as far
as horses can travel, a company has had enterprise enough
to build a footwalk, of boards on irons, along the face of
the perpendicular rock, in many places directly over the
yawning chasm, down which the water plunges and foams
a thousand feet or more. For seeing this great natural
show a franc is charged, and the company possibly do all
they can to keep their walks and steps in safe repair, but
in many places they are frail structures, and show signs of
decay, as the boards are kept constantly wet by the spray—
where the sun has not shone for a thousand centuries.

27.—The journey from Martigny to Chamony over the Tete-Noir Pass, by carriages or mules, is tedious, and in many places dangerous, and much the worst road I have seen in Europe. The whole day is required to make the trip, though the distance is probably not over twenty-five miles. I would advise all young men who think of making this journey to do so on foot as they will certainly be obliged to walk a part of the distance at any rate, and pay ten dollars for their passage besides. Then they can make the trip in much less time than is required by these mule teams, and do so with safety, even without a guide, though it would be best to not go alone as in case of accident or robbers. This day was dark, cold, and misty, and we at one time rode through the clouds, it was interesting to see them form and float away around and below you, but I felt no desire to take a ride on one of them—thought for safety over these mountain crags I should prefer a mule. Chamony is not a large town, it consists principally of mountains and cascades, but people flock here to enjoy the fine scenery and to escape the heat of summer, and the latter they do effectually for fires and overcoats are indispensible to day; but who would not imagine he was cold when every time he looked from his window he could see mountains of snow and ice, though it might be, as it is, miles away; but then the quantity makes up for the distance, and after looking at it for a few minutes, I instinctively punch the fire and call for more wood.

28.—Looking at the glacier of Mt. Blanc to-day, I concluded to go there, supposing it might be a mile or two, but after walking for half an hour or more it seemed to be

as far away as when I started, but keeping on over deep
gulches on slender footwalks, beneath which the cascades
from the melting snow above plunged and thundered, along
winding paths through pine forests, upwards and still upwards, for over an hour, I at last came to the brink of the
gorge which seems to be a deep groove cut in the mountain
side near its base, this is probably a quarter of a mile in
width, and a hundred feet deep, getting wider as it ascends
until there seems to be nothing but a mountain of snow or
ice, just as white, resembling in its fantastic shapes an ice
gorge on some great river.   As this thaws away from below,
the heavy body of snow and ice above, having no support,
slides down ; this is the dreaded and dangerous avalanche
of which no conception can be formed without seeing the
magnitude of this unparalelled ice-cream freezer—miles
in extent, and thousands of feet in height, so far above the
clouds that no one but an idiot would think to ascend ; it
is nearly 16,000 feet in hight, 8,000 being about the snow
line, so that some 8,000 feet of this mountain is perpetual
snow and ice.   I am told that out of the thousands that
attempt its ascent every year, only about fifty reach the
top, and that of these one-half never return alive.   Water
enough is constantly flowing down its sides from the melting snow to turn the machinery of the world, the noise
from which is not like the heavy dull roar of Niagara, but
like that of a spring thaw when all the streams are swollen.
This is Mt. Blanc, fearfully and awfully grand ; the rains
and suns of countless summers have failed to melt or
soften its icy heart ; what little impression they make during the few months of summer is overcome by the snows

of winter, and so they will never all melt till the " crack
of doom."

29.—This morning a large party started, as on every
fair day, for the *Mer-de-Glace*, or sea of glass, and Mauvais
Pass.   This mountain from which these are viewed and
crossed is not so high and more easy of access than Mt.
Blanc, and as the trip can be made in one day, while the
ascent of the latter requires three, in case you live long
enough to make it at all, many prefer the shorter journey.
This is made with mules, price of each, six franks ; guides
are plenty who propose to lead your mule for six franks
more, then they tell you it is impossible to get along without a long stick with a pike in the end, for the use of
which they charge one-half frank ; then they sell you for a
frank a pair of socks to wear over your boots to prevent
your slipping on the ice, though they are so thin and worth-
less that three steps generally tear them all to pieces.   Thus
equipped and mounted with six little sheep bells dingling
from the old blind bridle, a fool to each mule, and sometimes two, we start on our journey looking like a caravan
of Arabs on the desert.   The day was fine, not a cloud in
sight, the high white mountain peaks glistened in the bright
sunlight like tall monuments in the city of the dead.   The
distance to the head of *mule navigation* is probably five
miles, the path for the greater part of the distance is ser-
pentine, and through a pine forest on the mountain's side·
It is not necessarily dangerous, and yet lives are often lost in
making the journey.   On this occasion, shortly before reaching the top, we came upon a number of persons by the roadside surrounding the body of a large man to whom they

were attempting to give some stimulant. I immediately
dismounted, and upon going to the spot found the man was
dead. As none of his companions could speak English, it
was difficult to get at the facts in connection with his death,
but from his appearance I inferred he had been subject to
epilepsy, that the fatigue of the journey, and great elevation had induced an attack causing him to fall amongst
the rocks, producing concussion of the brain from which
he died. The crossing of the glacier, the mer-de-glace,
with a good guide, is neither difficult or dangerous, while
that of Mt. Blanc is both; the ice is as white as the driven
snow, and very hard, in some places crevices several inches
wide are observed, such as occur in large rocks; how deep
these may be there is no means of knowing, they are
usually filled with clear ice-cold water as all the water flowing from these glaciers is; but the fall being so great over
the rocks, and a kind of gray soft gravel, by the time it
reaches the larger streams in the valleys it in color and
appearance resembles soap-suds. All the large streams
here are of this character, and they foam and dash through
their rocky beds with a current perfectly fearful.

30.—The journey from Chamony to Geneva, a distance
of fifty miles, is made by diligence; the road is safe and
good, and for the greater part of the way there can be no
good reason why a railroad should not be built. Geneva
is a pretty city, of 50,000 inhabitants, situated on the river
Rhone in a delightful valley, with mountain peaks in the
distance; amongst which the bald head of Mt. Blanc is
still conspicuous, and as the rays of the setting sun are
reflected from its summit, and it retires behind the western

hills, it seems discouraged that while for ten thousand centuries it has warmed and invigorated all else in nature, it has shone here to little purpose. A good deal of enterprise and modern taste are exhibited at Geneva, and English is spoken in shops, hotels, and offices more generally than at any city, perhaps, on the Continent; besides the citizens dress with more taste, and the ladies look more civilized. It is a delightful summer residence, and many come here for this purpose. How the climate may be other seasons I have no means of knowing, but at this time it is quite cool, so that winter clothing and fires are not at all uncomfortable. The manufacture of watches and musical instruments, particularly music boxes, seems to be the prinpal trade of Geneva; some of the latter are very fine, and vary in price all the way from $2.00 to $500. They have musical writing desks, musical bottles, and even chairs that play when any one sits on them.

31.—They show you the old church here where John Calvin preached, and the house where he lived. Whether he could be considered a reformer, or whether the doctrine he preached was any improvement on that he condemned, is a matter of opinion. Such men as he, Robert Knox, and Martin Luther, get people to thinking, and the agitation of thought is the beginning of wisdom, though change is not always progress or improvement.

September 1.—The country from Geneva to Berne is probably the best part of Switzerland. The distance is 150 miles, and the scenery up the beautiful blue lake of Geneva is very fine. Berne is not so large or so pretty as

Geneva; population probably 40,000. It is the capital of Switzerland, and apart from this has for the sight-seer little of interest. The day was dark, cold, and wet, and, as some of our party seemed not to know what we had stopped there for, I suggested that it might have been to sleep, as the place seemed to be a success for this purpose. Still the hotels were full of guests. English and Americans keep up these cities in the summer. How they subsist during their long winters I do not care to stay to find out. The climate at this season of the year is pleasant enough, but the cooking is inexcusably miserable, and this seems universal all over the Continent. There is one dish that appears more common than all others; it consists of *empty plates.* I should think about five hundred of these are required at every dinner for a small party. When will they learn anything?

2.—The first 25 miles from Berne to Interlacken is made by rail; then some ten miles by boat, on the beautiful Lake Thune; then again by railroad on curiously constructed, double-decked cars that carry as many passengers on top as inside, and besides gives them an opportunity to throw something at the engineer, if, in case of accident, they should want the train stopped; for nowhere in Europe, so far as I have seen, are there any bells on the locomotives, or any way for a passenger to signal an engineer to stop. The usual custom at a station is, after fussing for half an hour over baggage, (luggage, as they call it,) for a bell on the depot to be rung. Then some fellow blows a little dog-whistle; the engineer's whistle is then sounded, and the dog-whistle blows again; then the train starts, and you see no more of the conductor till it stops at the next station, unless he happens to crawl along the outside of the car and poke his head through the window, as they sometimes do, to ask for your tickets. You have no water, or any other accommodation more than in a common road-carriage, and not half as much, for the latter can be stopped at will—but this custom is all of a piece with most others. For instance, here, at Interlacken, they have a custom of taxing every guest that stops at a hotel half a franc every night because a band plays somewhere in their town; it makes no difference whether you hear it or not; they say you might have gone, and therefore have the ten cents to pay all the same. Their music is going on, I presume, now while I write, but I prefer to pay my dime for the privilege of staying in my room, for the night is wet and so cold that I write with two coats on, and am far from comfortable; but no wonder, when you can see snow on the mountains in every direction.

3.—Interlacken is not a city or even a large town, unless you count in the mountains; it is a small village of *hotels*, very pleasantly situated in a narrow valley between the lakes Thune and Brienz. It seems to derive its support principally from tourists who resort here to escape the heat of summer; and this we are certainly doing to-day, for it is not only cool, but cold, requiring a good fire, about which there seems to be quite a lively competition for seats. What will become of these hotels in the winter it is hard to conjecture, guess they will have to be closed, and their proprietors go to hunting the chamoise goat on the mountains. It would seem as though this was a great business here, for

they show you more chamoise horns than there are goats
in Switzerland; think they have some way of manufacturing these, and if you do not know the false from the
genuine, they answer every purpose; they have them on
canes, umbrellas, and toys, and yet you rarely see any of
the little animals that furnish so many bushels of these
horns.

4.—After two days rain this morning was bright and
clear, and the snowy peaks of the Bernese Alps glisten in
the sunlight like crystal palaces of some Magi of the upper
air. We start in carriages to visit the wonderful glacier of
Grindelwald. After a three hours ride up a beautiful valley, with high mountains and cascades on every side, we
leave our teams and ascend the mountain still further on
foot. The ice seems to be close at hand, but it requires a
tiresome walk of an hour to reach it. This appears clearer
and harder than that of Mt. Blanc, but here as there, some
enterprising genius, with an eye to business, has run a
tunnel, some eight feet high and six wide, a hundred feet
or more into the solid ice, and lit it up with lamps, and of
course charges you a franc for walking in ; he might just
as well have extended it a mile or two, for it would stand
a thousand years, unless an earthquake broke it to pieces.
Why don't he start an ice cream saloon in there? The ice
would cost nothing, and goat's milk is plenty in the valley;
but the Switzer, like the Italian, thinks more about his wine,
beer, and sour bread. The Italian cuts a slice of this, feeds
it to his mule, and then helps himself; I had formerly
thought a mule had some sense, but when I saw him eat
that bread, I lost all confidence in his judgment; an ostrich

might possibly eat it, if he had been a week without a good square meal of glass and old iron, but it looks bad for a mule. Ladders could be had here to climb the glacier, and anyone who wished, could break his neck, for a small fee; but for my own part, having but one neck, the inducement did not seem sufficient to make the exchange; besides, I had seen about enough of glaciers to last me the balance of my life; and if I should ever encounter excessive heat anywhere, I shall think of the days spent on these ice mountains, and defy sunstroke. A few hours later to-day, a young Englishman, by the name of Latham, lost his life here by falling into a deep gorge, and his body was not found till next morning.

5.—The joruney from Interlacken to Lucerne is made by railroad, steamboat, and carriages. The scenery is lovely, mountains, valleys, lakes, and cascades, all combine to make the Brunning Pass unequalled in Switzerland. All day long you never lose sight of snow and ice, in some places a thousand feet in thickness, and in others only in isolated drifts in the mountain gorges, but the sight of this, together with the jingle of sleigh-bells, a string of which the driver never fails to put on every horse, reminds one of mid-winter, though the sun may be shining warm and bright in the valleys. Ten hours were required to make this journey, and, as the day was fine, it was one of the most pleasant spent in Europe.

6.—To-day we ascend the Righi, a high mountain in sight of Lucerne, but really eight or nine miles distant; we reach its base by steamer on the lake, and its top by

open cars pushed up an incline plane of four inches to the
foot by a curiously constructed locomotive. The grade is
fearfully steep, and it throws a chill over the passenger
on looking out to see if the car is suspended in mid air, or
resting on something permanent. For three or four weeks
I had schooled myself in looking down deep gorges and
chasms, but my courage was taxed to its utmost here by
sometimes not being able to see any bottom. The road,
however, seems to be well built, and accidents rarely occur.
The Righi is not quite 6,000 feet in height, and, therefore,
below the snow line; but being almost surrounded by lakes,
the fine view from its top is unobstructed by other mountains, and is superlatively lovely. This is a great place
for tourists. The hotels at the summit furnish accommodations for several thousands, and in the summer they are
well patronized; but during the long winters they, as well
as the road, must be dead stock. Many stay over night
here to see the sun rise, but as it is cloudy, misty, or rain-
ing two days out of every three, very few are gratified·
When the clouds and mist clear away the lakes appear as
green as the foliage that covers the mountains. Cities and
hamlets deck the valleys that stretch miles on miles away,
with snowy Alpine peaks in the back ground, and as the
bright sunshine like a calcium light is thrown on the
picture below, it is like the changes of the kaleidoscope,
or the phantom visions of a fairy land. One thing that
attracted my attention in this mountainous region was the
number and variety of beautiful flowers. Why do they
select this cold chilly atmosphere to

  * * * * "blush unseen,*
 And waste their sweetness on the desert air?"

Do they prefer to live, and even if need to die in retire-
ment, unless some one should come who could appreciate
them? Here is that strange white velvety star-shaped
flower, if flower it can be called, the Edelweiss; it evidently belongs to the family *immortalis*, and is never found
I believe, except in the vicinity of perpetual snow. They
appear to be held in high estimation, and are gathered by
the peasants and sold to the *innocents* for a franc each—of
course we invested. The Eye-bright (*Euphrasia officinalis*)
is very numerous, as well as the low evergreen shrub called
Ling, that much resembles the Scotch heather, but it is not
so tall, and in places covers acres of the mountain sides
with its little purple flowers. These, and many others that
seem to be indigenous to these mountain crags, lend their
variegated tints to embellish for the eye of the wanderer,
these pictures in nature's gallery.

7.—Lucerne, as well as the surrounding mountains and
valleys, is filled with traditions of William Tell and Arnold
Winkelried. They have also a very good representation
of a dead lion 28 feet in length, cut out of the solid rock, in
commemoration of the Swiss guard who fell in defending
Louis XVI against the mob at Paris in 1792. A high
rugged mountain, rising abruptly from the lake, is called
Pilate, and there is a tradition that Pilate left Judea and
wandered to this mountain, from the top of which he com-
mitted suicide by plunging into the lake.

> And still it is said, when day hath fled,
>   And moonbeams gild the night,
> His spirit walks, and wildly talks,
>   Upon this giddy height.

This story does well enough as a legend, but the man who believed it died many years ago and left no descendants. The stories of Tell and Winkelried are somewhat better authenticated, though no doubt greatly exaggerated. Still it is not at all surprising that an ignorant and superstitious peasantry, in a country so wild and romatic, should have many legends as wild as their mountains. But to-morrow I leave Switzerland, with its vine-clad and snow-capped mountains, its blue lakes, cascades, and honest simple-minded people. How they lived years ago, before tourists came amongst them, is hard to comprehend, since so much of their support now appears to come from this source. Stage, railroad, and steamboat lines are in the trade of carrying passengers alone, and all classes are more or less interested. The country, as a cold, rocky, mountain region, is a success, but for agricultural purposes it is and must forever remain a complete failure.

· **8.**—This morning we leave Lucerne for Paris, the journey is long and tiresome, requiring sixteen hours. We pass the lake and plain of Simpax where under the oaks

" The Switzers knelt in prayer."

We bid good-bye to the Bernese Oberland, whose white peaks still glittering in the sunlight are fading from view, but not from memory. So unlike the rest of earth, so like the moon, cold, barren, desolate, and majestic in their dignity, their impress will fade only as life fades into a dreamless sleep. The country here is much the best, and the best cultivated of any yet visited in this part of Europe, though this may be owing to the fact that it is more susceptible to cultivation. The farms are larger, or, at least, seem to be; but as no fences are observed, it is difficult to judge of their size, I should think, however, they were much large than those of Switzerland, where, if a farmer should slip on his steep mountain side, as he is constantly liable to do, he would be likely to fall from his own farm into the lands of his neighbor. We arrived at Paris at eleven o'clock at night too tired to think of anything but sleep.

9.—We rode all day through the streets of Paris, visiting its places of interest. In regard to its beauty, it depends entirely on taste, while no one will deny that it is a beautiful city. One might like Edinburg better, or another Florence, but take a part of these two cities, add the wide streets of Washington, some of the narrow ones of Brussels, Rome, or Naples, and a portion of the manufactures of London, and you have Paris, so that all tastes may be suited, either as it regards the city itself or anything that money can buy. One of the places visited was the tomb of the first Napoleon. No other man ever carved such an one with his sword, and certainly none with the pen. It is questionable if M. Thiers did not do much more for France, yet he lies in a modest family vault at Pere-la-Chaise, though it is said his remains are to be moved soon to the Pantheon. In another part of this cemetery, the most wonderful in the world, but which will soon have to be abandoned as a place of interment, a large sepulchre is conspicuous as being that of Abelard and Heloise. It is enclosed by an iron railing, inside of which, on its four sides, are beds of blooming flowers. The city probably

keeps these in such a fine state of cultivation, and for the
same reason, too, that crowds of tourists visit the place,
because of the romance connected with these names that
has followed them down through the uncertainties of 700
years. " Here," said the guide, " is the tomb of the two
greatest lovers of the world." But I thought that thousands, with as much love, and less heartless selfishness, have
since lived and died ; many who—

> Never told their love,
> But let concealment, like a worm i' the bud,
> Prey on their damask cheek.

They sleep in every church-yard, and yet no spacious
monuments mark the resting place of these life's heroes.

10.—As we had spent some weeks in Switzerland, viewing nature in her unbroken wildness, the cathedrals and
art galleries of Italy had been quite forgotten, but Paris
duplicates the whole thing. Notre DaméChurch, built some
700 years ago, and in which Napoleon and Josephine were
married, is, even for this age, a fine piece of architecture,
but then building expensive churches and castles was about
the only thing the ancients excelled us in. This was well
illustrated to-day on visiting the Museum of the Louvre
and Luxembourg Gallery. In the former is one of the
finest collections of paintings by Rubens, Murrillo, Vero-
nese, and other " old masters," to be found in the world, as
well as sculpture so ancient that no author is known, but
the exhibition of modern art in the latter, to my mind, as
far surpasses them as " daylight doth a lamp." But how
their colors will compare in three or four centuries, time
will have to determine. I said anything could be had for

money in Paris; yes, even horse meat. I saw a horse
butcher-shop to-day, and not a "one-horse" shop either,
but where nothing but horse meat is sold. Some of the
party invited me to go in with them and have some ordered
for lunch, but I did not feel just then as though I wanted
any lunch; guess the idea was all-sufficient. It may be all
well enough, but some way I concluded to stick to hard-
bread breakfasts and *table d'hote* dinners, as mean as they
are, a few days longer. The Commune, ten years ago,
played havoc with Paris. The Column Vendome has been
rebuilt, but some of the finest public buildings in the city,
or in the world, were totally destroyed, and are still ruins,
their charred and naked walls alone being left.

11.—I walked up the Champs Elysees to-day, which
leads from the Tuileries Gardens to the Arch de Triumphe,
a distance of nearly two miles. As a drive, a street, or a
walk, it is probably unequalled in the world. It was built
by Napoleon at a cost of over $2,000,000. The Arch,
occupying very high ground, and being itself 150 feet in
height, gives from its top a very fine view of the great city
that spreads out in every direction. Radiating from this
point, like so many spokes in a wheel, are fourteen wide
streets, boulevards, and avenues, each with from two to
four rows of shade trees, and dotted all over with thousands
of moving vehicles that look in the distance like so many
flies on a window. I am never fascinated with anything
at first sight, but like Paris better the more I see of it, and
much better than its weather. We had dust in Italy, snow
in Switzerland, and rain here. If they had as great a
variety in weather as in streets and shops, anyone might be

suited, but in this and in cooking the city seems to be a failure. We hear a great deal of talk in America about French cooking. Well, it is something to talk about; but any Western farmer's wife can get up a square meal that would make a French cook ashamed of himself, and this is pretty hard to do. She may not be so efficient in shuffling plates, or uncorking wine-bottles, but she will cook a meal that would satisfy any *human* appetite while he would be arranging his napkins and dishes. One of our party remarked that some hotel-keepers in New York were trying to adopt the French style of cooking, as well as the European *table d'hote* dinners. I told him I would run much faster to such a man's funeral than to put out a fire in his hotel.

12.—Paris differs in many respects from any other city on either continent. Its buildings are lower and more uniform. There are more tall houses on one street in Naples, or Chicago, than can be found here altogether, and there are very few red brick buildings in the whole city. The material of which the houses are constructed is probably stone, or a yellowish brick finished on the outside with cement, or plaster resembling stone, and of a yellowish white color; some might object to this sameness, but the architecture is usually fine, and you hear many adjectives applied to the city, but all express much the same idea— beautiful, lovely, magnificent. The streets are principally paved with stone blocks, on which there seems to be a thin coating of cement that wears up with constant travel, and wet, into a thin paste, not deep, but very disagreeable on a wet day. I should judge this to be a dear market gen-

erally, and you do not meet with the staid, candid, square
dealing of the Londoner here; you must rely on your own
judgment, and if that is defective, it is best to buy as little
as possible, and never from anyone who cannot speak English, unless you have a good knowledge of French. They
post "English spoken" in their windows, but they do not
say where. I asked a clerk in French if he spoke English;
he answered me in English, "Not much," and this I found
was about the extent of his English and my French.

13.—This day was clear and fine, the first for nearly a
week, a large party of tourists visited St. Cloud, or as the
French call it *San Clue*, and Versailles. The former is no
longer the regal palace it once was. In 1871, when the
Germans were about to take possession of Paris, this place
was burned by the French themselves to prevent it from
falling into the hands of their enemies, it is still a ruin and
questionable whether it will ever be rebuilt as its was formerly. The parks and walks, however, are still kept in
fine condition, and the location gives a fine view of the
city some five miles distant. Versailles, some ten miles
further away, is to Paris what Windsor is to London,
though its grounds are more artistic. The Boulevard de
la Reine, though not so long as the seven miles drive at
Windsor, is more beautiful. The two rows of elm trees on
either side are so planted and trimmed as to represent innumerable arches of which the body of each tree serves as
a column. The Royal Palace contains one of the finest
collections of modern paintings in Europe. They principally represent the various battles in the wars of the first
Napoleon. Versailles is reached by carriages, by horse

cars, and by steamers on the River Seine. This stream is
wider than the Thames at London or the Tiber at Rome;
but like the latter is not navigable, except for boats of
very light draught. But I must leave Paris soon. Weeks
might be spent here with many objects of interest still unseen. For variety of beauty as yet no city on earth is its
rival; but it remains for the western continent to furnish
this, which it will do within the next century. But I am
off for Dieppe, London, and home.

14.—This morning the sun rose bright and clear over
the blue waters of the English Channel. I had heard so
much of the trip from Dieppe to New Haven that I had
learned to dread it, but on this occasion the water was as
calm and still as an inland lake, and by twelve o'clock
we have passed the examination in the custom-house which
here consists pretty much of making a chalk mark on the
baggage. How is this: Can these officers detect a smuggler
at sight; if not, why do they scrutinize some luggage so
closely and pass others without a word? They were looking
principally for spirits, tobacco, and cigars they said. I told
them I never bought a cigar in my life, a plug of tobacco,
or pint of whisky, and they concluded I was safe. The
country from here to London contrasts finely with what
you see on the continent. The neatly trimmed hedges,
the cattle grazing without a tether or herdsman, the farm-
houses, barns, and orchards suggest the idea that by some
mysterious means we have suddenly crossed the Atlantic
and are traveling in America. But the smoke and spires
of London are soon visible, and why should they not be?
How can you travel towards it one hour from any point in

6

England and not be within sight of it? I have thought
it was only a matter of time when this city would cover
the whole island, and London be England as Paris is
France. But I leave this great empire city to-night for
Glasgow, and to-morrow hope to hear the "wild waves
saying"—"homeward bound."

15.—A night's ride from London brought me to Glasgow
at eight o'clock this morning in a dense fog, making it
difficult to navigate the streets much less the Clyde. Our
ship, the Anchoria, sails from Greenock this p. m. at five
o'clock, and passengers go there by rail, in this way some
two hours of time are saved, and often much more, with
heavy vessels and low tides. So this is my last day in
Europe, and though I have formed some agreeable ac-
quaintances that I regret to part with, and seen much that
was beautiful both in nature and art; the country itself I
leave with no regret; it may be a law of our nature that
while the young may be easily fascinated by change and
new scenes, those of more nature age are less disposed to
part with old for new homes; on the same principle, too, old
countries adopt new customs much more slowly. There is
a certain amount of courtesy due to age, and I, therefore,
very respectfully bid this old country good-bye, extending
at the same time to all of its citizens a hearty invitation to
call and see us. We can find homes for you all, feed and
clothe you all, and, what is little less important, educate
you all. But Greenock is reached, it was to this city on
that dark autumn day when—

> The gloomy night was gathering fast,

that Burns had sent his trunk preparatory to sailing for

the West Indies, and from which he was dissuaded by his
friend Cunningham, who saved him to Scotland.　In an
old church-yard here, overlooking the Clyde, is the grave
of Highland Mary.　This, to my regret, I am obliged to
pass without stopping, as the setting sun and the dark
cloud of smoke from the steamer in the frith admonish me
there is not time, and that in a few minutes more we will
again be " on the wide open sea."

16.—This morning our vessel is lying-to off the north
coast of Ireland ; the day is calm and the sea as smooth as
a mirror.　All day long we stay here, and the ride is as
smooth as in a sled without horses.　At three o'clock a
tug from Londonderry comes in, loaded with Irish, most of
them steerage passengers, for America.　Many are in families, and some have young children.　No wonder they
desire to take them to a better country, where their future
will be brighter and their advantages increased.　We have
65 saloon passengers on board, of whom one-half are
Americans returning home, and about 800 second-cabin
and steerage passengers.　The last rocky cliffs of "Auld
Ireland" are fast fading from view, and the wide Atlantic
lies before us, where for many days we shall hear nothing
of what occurs on land, and no one will hear of us.　Many
sails dot the horizon, looking like chandeliers hung from
the sky.　The evening is chilly, too cold for comfort on
deck, but I presume this is customary here ; in fact, they
report at Glasgow there have been but a very few warm
days during the entire summer, and of over eighty days
since leaving New York there have not been more than
twenty that I have not been cold with winter clothing and
heavy overcoat.

17.—Day clear, with a high, cold wind; the sea is rough, and most of the passengers are sick. Some vessels appear to be steadier than others with the same sea, though this may, in a great measure, be owing to the direction of the wind. It is not surprising that ours is a little shaky, since it has 300 barrels of whisky on board, enough certainly to make most things reel. The whistle is sounded a great deal to-day; I don't know why; I can see nothing on the track, and there is no fog, bridges, or tunnels. Too cold to be on deck, so I stay below; have a strange genius for my room-mate—a young Scotchman, who has never been to sea before, and I guess nowhere else much, is going to America to find his brother.

18.—Dark and damp, with high, cold wind; the sea is rough, and our old ship rocks like a bird's nest on a bough; it rolls from side to side till the wheels miss the water, rattle and crash as if breaking to pieces. Not one-third of the passengers report at table. I am satisfied sea-sickness depends much on the state of the stomach before and after going on board. Passengers should eat a light diet and keep quiet; a cup of Brand's extract of beef, quite hot, with a little salt and crackers; then lie down most of the time. This, with the properly-selected homœopathic remedies, will modify most cases and prevent many. All crude drugs and specifics for it are worse than useless. Take the advice of no one to walk or keep moving; you will get motion enough from the boat; keep as still as it will let you.

19.—Still cold and disagreeable, not stormy, but the

same high wind; the sun comes out at times, but much
like a November day; the sea is still very heavy; only a
few passengers come to their meals. If the entire voyage
continues so rough the ship's company will save a good
thing in the way of provisions. It is unsafe to attempt to
walk without support. I fortunately have a large, easy
chair fastened to the floor, and feel pretty secure. A lady,
in passing, misses her hold on the door, and brings up on
my knee, and the next minute she is piled up on the cabin
floor ten feet away. Another falls off her lounge, and goes
rolling over the floor·like a thistle-down. An old gentleman suddenly finds he has urgent business on the other side
of the boat, where he goes with such force as to break his
nose against the wall. Another, for safety, seats himself
on the floor. A gentleman attempts to assist a lady, and
they both fall over him. Of course the laugh comes from
the very few who feel like it. I see nothing but the direction of the wind for this tossing, as there is no storm; but
old Neptune is evidently disturbed about something; hope
he will calm down soon; our ship seems as though it would
go over.

20.—Last night and to-day have been, if possible,
rougher than any of the voyage so far, and there seem to
be little prospect of its being any better soon; it is impossible to sleep, as it is difficult to stay in our bunks at all ;
no one thinks of going on deck; the waves dash over the
sides of the vessel and darken the windows. We have
now been out five days, and are about only one third of
the distance over, but it is hard to see how the ship can
make better headway in such a sea, besides we suffer from

cold, the heaviest winter clothing fails to keep us warm.
There is no fire, except in the cook-room where no one is
permitted to go. The bed clothing feels as if packed in
ice. It is safe to say two thirds of the passengers are sick,
and some have been badly hurt from falling. I still, during the day, keep my old chair, and suffer more from cold,
loss of sleep and appetite than anything else. I eat very
sparingly, and have experienced no nausea for two or three
days. If any one thinks he would fancy this kind of
thing, he can have my place for a first-class ticket on a
coal cart.

21.—Last night about 11 o'clock, the engine suddenly
stopped and the ship is drifting. What can be the cause? I
lie still for half an hour and wonder, has it struck, is it leak-
ing, on fire, and a number of other agreeable conjectures
pass through my mind. My room mate is soundly sleeping,
I conclude not to wake him, thinking if we were going to
the bottom I envied his unconsciousness. Not feeling particularly sleepy just then, I got up and found most of the
passengers out, some had been on deck, and reported we
had had a collision, our vessel had struck another, cutting
it in two and sinking it with all on board. The excitement
was intense, and the most prompt cure for sea-sickness I
had ever witnessed. What kind of craft it was or how
many were on board, we could not learn. A cry was heard
for help that they were sinking, and though a boat was
lowered and search made, not a trace, except a piece of
spar, could be found. In a few minutes all was over, and
nothing could be heard but the dashing of the breakers
where—

The death angel flapped his broad wings o'er the wave.

Whether it be from law, custom, or humanity, under such circumstances, we are obliged to stay here till daylight to see if anything further may be learned; but the morning revealed nothing; a large hole had been stove in our ship, into which the water poured, filling the chamber, but as these chambers are watertight it could not reach any other part of the ship, and this of course saved us from going down also. By eight o'clock we were again on our way, but making slow progress, against a head wind and heavy sea. It is fearfully grand to see these mad breakers foam and dash their white heads into spray; I admire nature in her wildness, but believe I prefer burning or ice-covered mountains to this, unless I could view the sight from some hilltop where there would be less danger of getting wet.

22.—After another fearful night the sun rose bright and clear this morning, and we congratulated ourselves we had seen the worst of the voyage, but the wind kept up, and the sea was heavy; towards night it became rainy, and the wind increased. Have now been out one week and are only about half way over. I had always regarded a storm at sea as something to be dreaded, but find it is not necessary there should be a storm in order to insure a rough passage. The fact is to be angry and fretful, is old ocean's normal condition, and when it is not so it is not healthy; and one of its worst features is, when it gets in a fury it never knows when to calm down again. Very few vessels are seen to-day, perhaps we are the only fools out, as people have a dread of the sea during the equinox, though the steamers make their regular trips all the same. We have only run one hundred and fifty miles in the past twenty-

four hours, about one-half of what we should have gone.
Still, there is no help for us, we can't get out and walk.
Another rough night is threatened ; sleep is much in de-
mand, with but little in the market.

23.—How are you feeling to day, has been the question
generally asked for the past week, and while some answer
" better," very few can say " all right ; " for if they are im-
proving physically, mentally, they are far from serene, for
the wind still blows a gale, and lashes the sea into a fury.
There seems to be no cessation day or night, if it would
only let up a few hours for us to sleep we could endure it
better.   But, who can sleep being tumbled and rolled and
tossed every minute.   I go on deck the first time for five
days to take a look at the situation, but the whistling of
the winds through the rigging, the roar and dash of the
breakers, and the rolling and dipping of the ship soon
cause me to retire in disgust.   The weather is much colder
than yesterday, and though we have made better time, one
hundred and ninety miles. We are still hundreds of miles
behind, and at best must be two or three days late in getting into port, if, indeed, we ever do ; and the unanimous
verdict amongst the passengers seems to be that in any
event this will be their last trip on the ocean.

24.—Though the wind is still high and cold, and the
sea rough, this is a decided improvement over any day for
the passed week.   We still have over a thousand miles to
go, but have made two hundred and thirty-eight in the

passed twenty-four hours, which is the best run with one exception since starting. We are now passing the banks of New Foundland, and hope soon to see fairer and warmer weather. What causes the peculiar bluish-green appearance of the water over these banks? Sailors say they notice this change whenever they approach them. Is it because the depth is not so great? There can be no difference certainly in the water itself, though it has more the appearance of an inland lake than the ocean. Some of the passengers try to make themselves comfortable on deck, but it requires all the winter clothing and wraps they can command, for my own part I am cold in the drawing-room, with overcoat and winter gloves on; but there is one consolation, we are not at all troubled with mosquitoes. A few of Mother Carey's chickens are to be seen; what a strange bird, they seem to require no land, must live entirely on what they find in the water, on which they float like a chip, but whether they rest most on the wing or on the billow, who can tell?

25.—One fair day at last; the wind has abated, the sun is out, and so are the passengers, enjoying the *scenery* which consists principally of the steamer Anchoria, the sun, sky, and water. It only takes a few minutes to see all these, and as we had seen them all before, except the warm sunshine, and smooth sea, we appreciate these. We have made over 300 miles in the past twenty-four hours, and begin to talk of getting home in three days more. The sailors put up all their canvas, and the wind is in our favor; no sails in sight to day, but a piece of timber floats by that probably once belonged to a vessel of some kind that may have gone down in the wide expanse of waters, How many have thus perished in the past ten days, time only can determine; or how many friends at home are patiently waiting their return, and wondering at the delay, but—

> Days, months, years and ages will circle away,
> And still the deep waters above them will roll.

26.—Another fair day, though the wind is ahead, and in consequence, our progress is slower, only 192 miles since yesterday, and are now making less than twelve miles an hour, but we don't complain of the speed, or the fact that we are so far behind time, but rather rejoice that we are doing so well after our rough experience, and as the weather is so pleasant we get together on deck and have readings and songs, and near the drawing-room door is posted the following—

NOTICE.

There will be an entertainment this evening, at 8 o'clock, in the music-room, for the benefit of the " Life Boat." All are invited.

Then follows a programme, with the following names for readings, recitations, and music, vocal and instrumental: Mr. Olandt, Mr. McDougal, Mr. Croffut, Dr. C. Pearson, Mr. Baer, Mr. Donald, Mr. Sweeney, Misses McClain, Swan, and Moul. No admission fee is required, but each one is expected to contribute something toward the life-saving service, and if there be any cause in the world that deserves assistance it is this.

27.—Our entertainment last night was quite a success, and a good sum was realized for the life-boat service, which it seems in Europe is supported mainly by contributions and donations. May our mite recompense, in some degree, those daring fellows that brave the perils of the waves to save the lives of others. The fog to-day and last night is against us; still we have made 290 miles in twenty-four hours ending at noon to-day, and are still 278 from our destination, which we expect to reach to-morrow afternoon. Passengers are busy writing letters to papers and friends, probably describing their rough passage and narrow escape. Some who had crossed the ocean seven times say they never experienced such a passage as this, and a few days ago declared if they got through this time in safety, nothing would ever tempt them to try it again. But they are feeling better to-day, and very likely, in a few years more, we will see their names registered in Paris.

28.—Morning clear, but wind high and sea rough again, and to such an extent that some of the passengers have a return of their old comforter, sea-sickness. At ten o'clock the captain tells us we can see land, and if we cannot, it is not because we do not want to; of course we are willing to admit it is in sight, but it takes a good share of imagination to perceive it. An hour or two later, however, the coast comes full in view, and, except on the night of the disaster, when sick men run up on deck, I have never seen a more potent or permanent cure for any disease of thirteen day's duration. We reach New York at 2 o'clock p. m., and I cross the ferry to Jersey City, but in doing so our boat collides with another, and I wonder if these col-lisions will cease when I cease to travel. Took train for Washington, where I arrived at 11 o'clock p. m. Glad I had gone, glad I had returned. Should any one ask my opinion of this trip as a sanitary measure, I can only say "try it;" for my own part I return fourteen pounds lighter than when I left; perhaps I am so indigenous to American soil as to not thrive on any other.